"Does that mean you forgive me?"

Cort's voice was soft. Dangerously so.

Reluctance delayed Laura's reply. She had no doubt he regretted the harsh way he'd broken off their affair, but she sensed some hidden challenge in his gaze. "Yes, I forgive you."

He slipped his hands around her waist and pulled her slowly, determinedly, into a hug. She was once again aware of his strength, his muscled hardness, the achingly familiar scent of his hair and skin. He took her mouth in a deep, moving kiss.

Desire flared between them, hot and swift. The very intensity of that tripped some internal alarm, and sanity rushed back.

She pulled free of him, her heart slamming against her rib cage. "Why did you *do* that?" she whispered frantically between erratic breaths.

His eyes burned bright. "For the same reason you didn't stop me." His reply shook her almost as much as his kiss. "Tell me, Laura," he commanded gruffly, "why didn't you stop me?"

Dear Reader,

Harlequin Temptation celebrates its fifteenth birthday this year! When we launched in 1984, our goal was to be the most sensual, most contemporary series in the marketplace. Today we're still that—and *more*. Each month we bring you four fun, sexy stories that range from romantic fantasy to "Blazing" sensuality. Temptation is *the* series for women of the new millennium.

Over the years popular authors such as Jayne Ann Krentz, Barbara Delinsky, LaVyrle Spencer and Carla Neggers have contributed to the success of Temptation. Many of our writers have gone on to achieve fame and fortune—and the *New York Times* bestseller list!

In celebration of our fifteen years, I'm delighted to introduce you to three shining stars. Say hello to Pamela Burford, Alison Kent and Donna Sterling, who are each thrilled to bring you their sizzling stories in September, October and November.

I hope you enjoy these talented authors, as I hope you will enjoy all the fabulous books and authors to come.

Happy reading!

Birgit Davis-Todd
Senior Editor, Harlequin Books

P.S. We love to hear from readers! Write and tell us what your favorite Temptation book was over the past fifteen years. We'll publish a list of the top fifty!

Harlequin Books
225 Duncan Mill Road
Don Mills, Ontario
CANADA M3B 3K9

THE DADDY DECISION
Donna Sterling

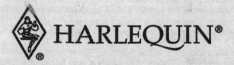

HARLEQUIN®

TORONTO • NEW YORK • LONDON
AMSTERDAM • PARIS • SYDNEY • HAMBURG
STOCKHOLM • ATHENS • TOKYO • MILAN • MADRID
PRAGUE • WARSAW • BUDAPEST • AUCKLAND

To those who brought so much fun to my life as I was growing up—my aunts and uncles. Ruth and Larry, Ann and Bob, Jane and Ed, Ronnie, Rita and Dana, Terry and Jerry, Al and Cheryl, Chris and Kate.
You've always meant more than you realize!

Also my thanks to
Mary Duke of Duke Design Associates
in Atlanta for her help, and
Susan Goggins, Carina Rock,
Jacquie D'Alessandro and
Anne Bushyhead
for invaluable critiques.

RECYCLED PAPER · RECYCLED PAPER

ISBN 0-373-25854-2

THE DADDY DECISION

Copyright © 1999 by Donna Fejes.

Visit us at www.romance.net

Printed in U.S.A.

Dear Reader,

As Harlequin Temptation celebrates its fifteenth anniversary, I'd like to express the joy it has brought me over the years as both a reader and a writer. Temptation novels allow me to savor the kind of romance that gladdens my heart and reaffirms the beauty of the profound bond between soul mates. I can't think of anything more thrilling.

Writing for Harlequin Temptation has also won me many of the industry's most prestigious nominations and awards. My heartfelt thanks to the editors of the Harlequin Temptation line, and a very "Happy Fifteenth Anniversary"!

And to you, dear reader, I wish many more years of happy romance reading!

Please feel free to visit my Web site at www.temptationauthors.com or e-mail me at donnasterling@mindspring.com, or mail me at P.O. Box 217, Auburn, GA 30011. I'd love to hear from you.

Yours sincerely,

Donna Sterling

Books by Donna Sterling

HARLEQUIN TEMPTATION
655—HIS DOUBLE, HER TROUBLE
694—THE PRINCESS AND THE P.I.
726—SAY "AHHH…"
738—TEMPERATURE'S RISING

1

THE MISCHIEVOUS GRIN on his sister's face as she met him at the door on that snowy Wednesday evening put Cort immediately on guard, but by the time she'd drawn him inside her Lake Tahoe chalet, the trap had already sprung.

An unexpected mob converged on him in the great room with exuberant greetings, hugs and handshakes.

He should have known better than to believe he'd be Steffie's only guest this Thanksgiving. Surrounding him were faces he hadn't seen in over a dozen years. Tension gripped him as he scanned those faces, searching for one in particular that had always been among them.

Laura Merritt.

She wasn't there. At least, not in the small, welcoming circle around him. He relaxed somewhat and returned the hugs and handshakes.

"Cort Dimitri, you old dog!" greeted B.J. Mayhew, the most radical feminist ever to raise a fist on the University of Georgia campus. "What were you thinking, staying out of touch with us for fifteen years?" Although her auburn hair was still as short as a man's and her voice nearly as gruff, she was dressed in a tweed blazer and khakis instead of her old braless tank top and jeans. "I don't care *how* rich you are now. I still ought to kick your butt."

"Yeah, you promised me that years ago," Cort replied, still tense from the surprise, "and I haven't seen any action yet."

A strong, mittlike hand gripped his and turned him toward a burly giant with skin the color of black coffee and a smile as wide as a goalpost. "Congratulations, man. Heard you sold your chain of sports bars for big bucks." Pumping his hand was Hoss "the Boss" Tucker, one of the hardest-hitting linebackers in UGA's history. A light sprinkling of gray glinted in his short black hair. "I go by 'Coach' now. Been shaping up the Prattsville Pirates for the past few years. Six-and-four for the season. Could have used some of your armchair quarterbacking."

"He wouldn't have listened to a word of it," cut in Tamika, looking and sounding exactly like the sassy cheerleader she'd been when Hoss had first brought her home. With her hair braided in her usual queenlike coronet, she held a sleeping baby in her sleek brown arms and wore a sizable diamond on her left hand.

"Hey, Cort, my man!" came a masculine shout from the far corner of the massive great room. The greeting was followed by an expressive squeal from an electric guitar. All eyes turned to the blond guitarist, who smiled happily as he made the instrument scream. Cort shook his head with a reluctant smile. "Rockin' Rory" Harper still had that damn guitar attached to him like an extra appendage. He'd put some meat on his bones and his hairline had receded, but his platinum hair was still pulled back in a ponytail, his handlebar mustache still drooped to his jaw and his faded jeans still sagged as if he'd just removed his stash of pot from their well-worn seat.

B.J. yelled at Rory to turn down the volume before he woke Tamika's baby, Tamika instructed Hoss to put the baby to bed upstairs, Hoss told Rory to play some Jimi Hendrix, and Steffie took the snow-dampened coat from Cort.

Cort, meanwhile, looked around again to assure himself

that no one hung back from the friendly ruckus in an attempt to avoid him. He braced himself for that possibility, half expecting to meet the gaze of the brown-eyed blonde he hadn't seen for fifteen years. She'd been such an integral part of this crowd that he couldn't believe she wouldn't be included.

"She's not here yet, Cort," his sister said, returning from the coat closet. "She should be soon, though."

He didn't pretend not to know whom she meant. Gritting his teeth, he tucked a firm hand beneath his sister's elbow and steered her to the relative privacy of the kitchen, fighting the temptation to strangle her.

Steffie had told him she'd be spending Thanksgiving alone if he didn't join her. Newly divorced, she'd sounded so pitiful over the phone that Cort had carved a few days out of his busy schedule and flown back from Italy.

He supposed he should have known better than to believe her sob story. For years she'd celebrated Thanksgiving with these people, her closest pals from college—the odd assortment of individuals who had once shared the big, drafty, off-campus house on Hays Street.

From backgrounds as varied as New England fishing towns to West Coast hippie communes to inner-city backstreets, the only things they'd all had in common had been the University of Georgia and their lack of family to visit during vacations. They'd banded together on those occasions, as well as in other times of emotional need, and eventually bonded into a nontraditional family of their own.

The Hays Street gang, as they'd become known in their little college town of Athens, Georgia.

Although Cort had owned the house on Hays Street and lived there with them for a while, he hadn't attended any of their reunions over the years. He'd never really felt a part of the group. He was only four years older than Steffie and most of the others, but he'd felt decades older, working to pay the bills and Steffie's tuition while the others attended classes, parties and ball games. He'd actually seen very little of his housemates.

Except for Laura.

Laura. Guilt and regret jabbed deep into his gut. He turned to his sister with a reprimanding gaze once they'd reached the kitchen. "Alone for the holidays, huh, Stef?"

"You *had* to come this time!" she declared in a forceful whisper. "Tomorrow will be our fifteenth anniversary celebration. Fifteen years since our first Thanksgiving together in the Hays Street house."

"So what does that have to do with me?"

Her dark eyes sparked with indignation in her pixielike face. "You don't have a sentimental bone in your body, do you?"

"Never saw much profit in sentiment."

She compressed her lips and shook her head, setting her chin-length, glossy black hair into motion. "That's exactly the reason I wanted you here. I'm worried about you. You've been too caught up in business for so many years, you've forgotten there's anything more to life. And now, with this new, high-flying life-style of yours, I'm more likely to see you on the news or on some society page than I am in person."

"That's crazy."

"Oh, yeah?" She lodged a hand on one hip. "How long will you be able to stay with me this time?"

"Until Saturday." After a reluctant pause, he admitted, "I have an important meeting in London first thing Monday."

She threw her hands up. "London, Japan, New York.

You're always with the 'power players' now. You've lost touch with the people who really care about you."

"Like who?"

"Me, for one. When was the last time we saw each other?"

"Just a few months ago."

"Twelve, Cort. A full year. And that was only because you had a two-hour layover. You can barely squeeze me in your schedule, you're so wrapped up in your financial ventures and schmoozing with high society." She shook her head again, looking bewildered. "How can you be happy spending so much time with the same kind of people who put us down our whole lives? Don't you remember what they did to Papa, and Mama, and...and us?"

"I haven't forgotten a damn thing." A surge of dark emotion accompanied the words. He would never forget. And that was why he intended to climb to the very top of the power chain. Nobody he cared about would ever again suffer the fear and degradation that had beaten down his Greek immigrant parents and riddled his and Steffie's childhood.

A weary sigh escaped her. "There's more to life than acquiring power, Cort. There's friendship. Family. Love. I know you believe in all that, or you wouldn't have bought me this house. All I'm asking is that you start using that heart of yours a little more—*really* using it—before it withers away."

He couldn't resist teasing her. "What, you want another house?"

She punched him in the shoulder. "I'm serious, Cort! I pray every night that you'll fall in love with some nice woman and marry her and start a family of your own."

"A family of my own?" Images of "family" flashed through his mind—his father slaving for a pittance to keep them sheltered and fed, until he doubled over on the factory floor with no one caring enough to call a doctor as he died. His mother being dragged away by INS agents, her eyes wide with fear for the children left behind. Steffie as a twelve-year-old kid, hungry and cold, depending on Cort for her very existence.

Start a family of his own? He'd just as well cut open his heart and let it bleed. "Don't waste your prayers, Stef," he murmured. "You're all the family I need."

Her smile looked wistful and sad. "Then at least admit that you need friends. Real friends. Everyone in the Hays Street gang cared about you long before you made your millions."

"I barely knew any of them."

"Of course you knew them! In fact, for a while there, I thought that you and Laura might—"

"I barely knew Laura, either," he interjected coolly.

It was the truth. Despite all the time she'd spent in his bed—stolen hours between her classes and his two jobs—he hadn't really known her. He hadn't known her favorite food, music or colors. Hadn't known her hobbies, interests or views on life. He wasn't even sure he'd known her major. And he hadn't given any of those things a thought until he'd left her far behind him.

No, they hadn't wasted much time on talk. Hadn't gone anywhere or done anything that didn't involve sex. But they'd had plenty of that. He hadn't been able to keep his hands off her. And she hadn't been able to say no. At least, not to him.

She'd been a virgin the first time he'd made love to her.

A deep, sharp pang assailed him again, and he turned away from Steffie in search of a drink. A strong one.

She stopped him near the kitchen door. "Laura and

Fletcher will be here soon. They'll be surprised to see you. I, uh, don't believe I told them you were coming."

He turned back to face her. "Fletcher?" He'd forgotten about the quiet, serious young man who had moved into the Hays Street house shortly before Cort had moved out.

"He and Laura are coming straight from an interior designers' seminar. Fletcher runs an antiques shop in Memphis, and Laura opened an interior design business in the same building. They're trying to save up enough money to actually buy the place."

"They're...a couple?"

"Heavens, no. Actually, I've sometimes wondered if Fletcher might be gay."

Cort didn't comment. He knew that others had wondered about Fletcher, too, but he never had. He'd been aware of Fletcher's very male interest in Laura from the first time the guy laid eyes on her.

She'd had that effect on most men. She'd glowed with the kind of striking beauty that turned all gazes her way. Waist-length blond hair; a slender but voluptuous body; endless legs; smooth, honey-gold skin that a man couldn't help wanting to touch. She'd been too damn beautiful to be real. But she *had* been real. And kindhearted. And vulnerable.

He never should have let her move into the house on Hays Street.

"Cort, will you please try to relax for the next few days and have a little fun, like we used to?"

He managed a slight smile. "Okay. And I'm sorry if I've neglected you." He slipped an arm around her and soberly met her gaze. "I'd protect you with my life, you know."

Her eyes misted. "I know that. But I don't need your protection, Cort. We're not on the mean streets anymore."

"And I intend to keep it that way."

She hugged him tightly. "Even if you hadn't insisted on putting all that money in my account, I'm earning a decent living now. My teacher salary is more than enough to pay my bills. All I need is for you to be happy."

Happy. He'd never given that concept much thought. Didn't sound all that profitable.

The doorbell rang, and Steffie's face brightened. "I'll bet that's Laura and Fletcher." She hurried away to greet the newcomers.

Cort remained in the kitchen and headed for the bottle of fine, aged brandy he'd spotted on the counter. As he chose a snifter from the cabinet, he heard a babble of cheerful greetings in the other room, and then Steffie's questions. *Where's Fletcher? Missed the flight! Catching a later one?*

So. Laura had come alone. For no clear reason, the idea pleased Cort. He paused with the bottle of brandy in his hand and listened closely to catch her low, soft voice among the others.

"Wait, Steffie, don't close the door. The cabdriver's bringing in my luggage." Her voice hadn't changed. Still as warm and lilting as a blossom-scented Georgia morning. "He's the sweetest old man. He wouldn't hear of me carrying my own bags, even though he's got the worst cold."

The purely feminine sound of her voice embraced Cort with nostalgic force, and his tension grew. In days gone by, the mere murmur of it had filled him with a keen, sensual anticipation. Like Pavlov's dogs, he'd responded every time, regardless of where he was or whom he was with.

He poured the brandy into his glass and noted with approval that he felt no keen sensual anticipation whatsoever.

Even so, he had no business being here. She wouldn't

want to see him any more than he wanted to see her. The memories between them were not all pleasant.

He made the drink a double.

Would the sight of her still pack the same punch, still send him reeling? In all his travels and dealings with the "beautiful people," no woman's beauty had ever affected him quite the way Laura's had. Of course, he'd been only twenty-two back then and accustomed to the grim streets of the inner city. She'd been eighteen, a precious hothouse flower from the wealthy Atlanta suburbs. Fifteen years of life would have brought about some changes in her, he was sure—and in his reaction to her.

After a fortifying swallow of brandy, he ventured toward the great room.

"Thanks for bringing in my bags, Howard," he heard Laura say from somewhere near the door. "I know you were already freezing behind the wheel...and then to get out in all that snow. What a bad night for your heater to break!"

Cort heard her, but couldn't see her because of the others surrounding the entrance foyer. Even Rory had set his guitar aside and edged forward, waiting with an air of anticipation for her attention.

And Cort remembered that it had always been this way, whenever she'd come home. He'd had to wait his turn.

"Oh, Howard, look at your hands!" she softly exclaimed. "They're beet red. Frozen solid." Cort imagined her enfolding the old cabdriver's hands in hers. She never had hesitated to touch. "Here, take these gloves. They're the stretch kind, so they'll fit." An irascible bluster of protest answered her. "Now, Howard," she admonished, humor seeping into her voice, "don't make me sic my friends on you."

"Take the gloves, Howard," ordered B.J. in her gruff, no-nonsense voice.

Steffie and Tamika started in on him, too. After a short while of all four women talking at once, the poor guy apparently gave in and took the damn gloves, because his tormentors allowed him to leave.

Cort stood in the kitchen doorway and watched the group move en masse toward the immense stone fireplace with its blazing fire. B.J. showed Laura a new tattoo on her forearm. Tamika assured Laura that she had brought the baby, who was sleeping upstairs. Hoss bragged that his three-month-old son already showed signs of aptitude for football.

And through it all, Cort hadn't caught a clear view of Laura yet. She was blocked from his sight by the others clustered around her.

The tension within him gradually rose to the level of frustration. He hadn't wanted to see her again at all, damn it. But since he'd been forced into her presence, he wanted to get the initial confrontation over with.

He wanted to see her. *Now.*

As if responding to his unvoiced impatience, Steffie drifted off toward the closet with Laura's fleece-lined jacket, B.J. dropped down into an armchair near the doorway where Cort stood, and Tamika settled onto the sofa with her husband, leaving Laura standing alone at the hearth with Rory.

Although he'd expected changes in her, nothing had prepared Cort for the actuality.

He wouldn't have recognized her. At least, not right away.

Her hair was darker—more of a burnished honey than the bright, striking blond of her youth. It was shorter, too—no longer cascading in thick, shiny waves to her waist, but reaching only halfway down her back and tied at her nape with a black scarf.

She'd lost weight. If the voluptuous curves he remembered still existed, he couldn't see much of them beneath her long, bulky black sweater. Her heart-shaped face also looked slimmer, with every graceful curve and hollow more pronounced.

She wore no makeup, as far as he could tell, and no jewelry other than small, gold-stud earrings. A major change. She'd always been glamour incarnate—wine-colored lip gloss; exotic, kohl-lined eyes; gold or silver dangling from her ears, wrists and throat, even when she wore jeans. Designer jeans, of course. Sleek-fitting. With heels.

She now wore loose gray slacks with flat, practical boots.

The difference went deeper than her appearance, though. He wasn't sure how he knew, but he did. Something inside her had changed. Gone was the tangible sexuality that had glowed from her like a force field. Gone was the arousing air of promise, of intriguing possibilities, that had radiated from her like a perfume.

She looked, very simply, like a slim, attractive blonde in her late twenties. Maybe early thirties. A soft-spoken schoolteacher, or a P.T.A. mom. Certainly no femme fatale. No pinup come to life. No living, breathing fantasy.

He stared in both utter disappointment and acute relief.

"I would have brought my old lady," Rory was telling Laura, "but she had a gig, singing at a club in L.A."

"Do you still find time for *your* music?" Laura asked.

"Hey, can Rockin' Rory's brownies make you grin? Hell, yeah, man. I finished recording that CD we talked about last time. All original material. B.J. drew the cover art."

"Oh, Rory, that's great!" She turned toward B.J. with uplifted eyebrows. "B.J., I didn't know that you—" Her words broke off, and she did a startled double take toward the kitchen doorway. Her lips parted. Her gaze locked with Cort's.

At last. Her attention was his. *About damn time.*

Everyone glanced their way, and a peculiar tension seemed to fill the room. He suddenly felt like an interloper, disturbing the serenity of their cozy little group. The big, bad wolf, poised to pounce on the sweetheart of the Hays Street gang.

She looked soft, feminine and vulnerable.

He had no damn business being there.

Cort couldn't quite summon a smile, but he managed a nod. "Laura."

A faint flush rose in her cheeks. "Cort."

"Good to see you again." He politely extended his hand, more out of habit than anything.

She glanced at it. After a tense pause, she slowly extended hers. "Good to see you, too."

They clasped hands.

But her hesitation had thrown him. Logically, he understood why she might hold a grudge and hesitate to acknowledge him. Logically, he knew he deserved it. On some other level, though, he reeled from the blow. She'd never resisted touching him before. Physical contact between them had always been freer than the air they'd breathed.

His sense of loss stunned him. How could he feel a loss now when he hadn't seen the woman in fifteen years? Hadn't touched her in all that time. Or held her. *Not even once.*

She'd hugged everyone tonight except him.

The feel of her hand clasped in his helped Cort regain his equilibrium. She had, after all, only hesitated to shake his hand. She hadn't refused. Her palm settled against his in a warm, cozy fit. Her skin felt pleasingly soft and petal-smooth; her grip firm and responsive.

The contrasts had always stirred him, he remembered: her soft femininity, her surprising strength. Her occasional shyness; her propensity for sensual indulgence. Slow, savoring indulgence, at that...

Memories swamped him, and he involuntarily tightened his grip. The light honey-gold of her skin against the dark bronze of his brought back flashes too visceral to be considered memories. He felt her pulse accelerate to a strong, vibrant rhythm. Ah, he remembered that rhythm. His body remembered.

She withdrew her hand, her color becomingly high. "I...I'm glad you got the chance to join us." She smiled, but he recognized the effort behind it. He noticed the stiffness of her posture and the slight elevation of her chin. "I'm sure Steffie's thrilled that you're here."

"You *know* I am!" His petite, vivacious sister stepped in between them and hooked her arms around their shoulders, forcing them into a rather awkward huddle. "You are two of the nearest, dearest people in my life," she said fervently. "I love you guys." She kissed Cort's cheek with a loud smack, then did the same to Laura's. "Nothing makes me happier than to have you both here."

At such close proximity and with Steffie's shining gaze shifting between them, they had little choice but to meet each other's gazes in a show of affability.

But Cort read the uneasiness in Laura's eyes.

He couldn't help a small, rueful smile. Mending their rift wouldn't be nearly as easy as his Pollyanna sister obviously hoped. But, what the hell. He was willing to give it a try.

For Steffie's sake.

She clearly wanted them to acknowledge their reconciliation in some way—with words, or a hug. He wasn't opposed to a hug. A brief, casual, token hug.

In a tactically brilliant move, though, Laura circumvented it. "Oh, Steffie, you know *we* love *you*, too! And I'm very happy to be here." She kissed Steffie's cheek and hugged her, effectively cutting Cort out of the intimate circle.

"Now," Laura said as she drew away, "is there anything I can do to help you get ready for tomorrow, Stef? Any celery or onions to chop, pies to bake, or turkeys to, uh, pluck?"

"No," Steffie replied, clearly disappointed by the less-than-satisfying results of her mediation attempt. "Everything's ready for tomorrow."

"Oh. Good. Well, then, if you'll excuse me..." her smile graciously included Cort "...I can't wait another minute to see my little godson again." Her smile grew dazzling as she turned to Tamika. "You don't mind if I peek in at him, do you? I promise I won't wake him."

Tamika rose from the sofa with a delighted grin and led Laura up the stairs.

Cort refused to let his gaze follow them. Instead, he took a deep, unsatisfying swig of brandy. Laura had definitely changed...and in a profoundly disturbing way.

He wondered how deep that change went.

He wondered what a man would have to do to find out.

I CAN GET THROUGH THIS VISIT, Laura swore to herself as she followed Tamika down the stairs, back toward the last man on earth she'd wanted to see. Not even the precious sight of Tamika's beautiful baby boy sleeping with such sweet contentment had been able to soothe her anxiety.

The shock of seeing Cort Dimitri again—*touching* him

again—had left her trembly, hot and dazed, as if she'd narrowly escaped a fatal accident.

He looked better than ever. His towering height and athletic build seemed more solidly muscular than she remembered, and his masculine presence more potent—a daunting realization, considering the fact that he'd always awed her. The years might have added a few lines beside his thickly lashed eyes and deepened the grooves beside his full, wide, inexplicably sensual mouth, but this only added to the rugged allure of his swarthy face. His thick hair gleamed with the same ebony highlights. His deep, smooth voice held the intriguing cadence of his early upbringing in Greece. And he exuded the cool aura of strength and command that had captivated her as a giddy teen.

She hadn't been surprised to learn that he'd made millions. He'd always been so...intense.

That hadn't changed, either. When he'd tightened his grip on her hand and his dark, midnight-blue eyes had directed that inner intensity at her, a swift, responsive heat had flooded her.

Her knees trembled as she descended the stairs behind Tamika. Her reaction was due to the surprise of seeing him again, she assured herself. A nostalgic flashback gone awry. Nothing she couldn't handle.

Why in God's name had Steffie neglected to tell her he'd be here? She couldn't possibly have known that Laura would have found an excuse not to come. Although Steffie and the others knew that she'd been hurt by Cort fifteen years ago, none of them realized how long it had taken her to get over him, or how hard she'd found it to start dating again. Her pride hadn't allowed her to share the extent of her pain with anyone.

That, however, was long ago. She'd been "over" Cort

for at least a decade. Looking back, she realized she'd merely been infatuated—not with the man himself, but with the physical side of their relationship.

Physical *side?* Ha! There hadn't been any other side to it. She'd been a sheltered, naive schoolgirl, intoxicated with her newly discovered feminine power over men. He'd been the sinfully attractive bad boy who'd introduced her to sex.

And what an introduction! He'd approached it with the same intense determination he did everything else, and with his usual inexhaustible attention to detail. Just remembering the passion he'd ignited brought a flux of heat to her stomach.

It was easy to understand why she'd taken the relationship for more than it had been.

The pain of her disillusionment was a distant memory now, but the lesson she'd learned remained an integral part of her. She would never again confuse sex with love. She would never again base life's more important decisions on either. And she would never again get too close to the dangerous, mesmerizing fire that was Cort Dimitri.

From a few stairs below her, Tamika tossed a glance back at Laura, then halted on the small landing between flights of stairs. "Laura, are you okay?"

"Me?" She stopped beside her in surprise. "I'm fine. Why?"

Concern glinted in Tamika's gaze. "I mean, with Cort being here."

Laura felt her face warming. Had her anxiety been that obvious? Everyone would think she was holding a grudge. Or, worse yet, that she hadn't gotten over him. Good Lord, what if *he* thought that? "Of course I'm okay with Cort being here!" she exclaimed. "Why wouldn't I be?"

Tamika frowned. "Oh, I don't know."

Laura forced a laugh and swatted her friend across the shoulder. "Don't be silly. It's nice to see him again."

Tamika narrowed her gaze, looking doubtful. After a moment, though, she shrugged and led the way down the last turn of stairs.

Laura uttered a silent prayer of thanks that Tamika had brought her to her senses. Why had she let Cort's presence shake her? No matter how attractive he might be or what he'd meant to her in the past, he certainly posed no danger to her now. She was a strong, mature woman who was very happy in the life she'd made for herself. She'd learned how to control her own destiny; chart her own course.

Cort Dimitri posed absolutely no threat to her.

And, by God, she would prove it. Steffie had been trying for years to get Cort involved with the group again and was obviously thrilled with his visit. Laura would not throw a damper on that visit by holding herself aloof.

Perhaps, in the grand scheme of things, this was a test to see if she really had grown enough to handle the next step she planned to take in life—the most important step of her entire future. If this *was* a test of her worthiness, she would pass it with flying colors.

She would extend her cordial friendship to Cort Dimitri.

If only her legs would stop shaking long enough to get her down these damn stairs.

"Be sure to have Steffie take you on a tour of the house," Tamika was saying as they neared the bottom of the stairway. "Four bedrooms, three luxurious baths—bigger than my *bedrooms*, you understand—a billiard room, a solarium with a hot tub that overlooks the most gorgeous mountain view...."

"I'll take you on the grand tour later, Laur," Steffie cut in, meeting them in the great room. "We don't have time for it now. Everyone's in my office, by the computer. Rory and B.J. have a surprise for us. They've been collaborating on this project all year."

"Project?" Tamika said. "What kind of project?"

"A collection of old photographs that they transferred to compact disc." Steffie ushered them past a spacious, granite-floored kitchen and other rooms that Laura barely had a chance to glimpse. "If you'll remember, B.J. was always sneaking up on us with a camera."

Tamika groaned at the memory. "How can we forget? We never knew what stellar moments of our lives would be immortalized."

"I believe we're about to view those stellar moments *now*," Steffie predicted.

Laura barely gave the matter a thought. She focused her thoughts instead on the task that lay ahead of her—interacting on a friendly, casual basis with Cort Dimitri. She would prove to everyone, including him, that she had long ago forgiven and forgotten everything that had gone on between them. As far as she was concerned, he was now just one of the gang.

Steffie gestured her into an office crammed with oak filing cabinets, bookshelves, a desk and a computer hooked up to a large television screen. Rory sat at the computer with B.J. on his lap, her arm negligently draped over his shoulder. Cort and Hoss—both tall, muscular men who took up an extraordinary amount of space in the small room—lounged in executive leather chairs, talking football.

"Come in, come in, the show's about to start," urged B.J. "Pull up a lap."

Pull up a lap. They'd said those words to each other often enough. For years the Hay Street gang had been casually sprawling across each other's laps, looping arms about each other's shoulders, celebrating in their own way the platonic closeness they had nurtured over the years. *Pull up a lap.*

Tamika draped herself across her husband. B.J. had already claimed Rory. Laura stood in dismay near the doorway.

Only one lap was left unoccupied.

Cort raised an affable gaze to Laura and Steffie, then held up his hand in a welcoming gesture, indicating his willingness to be sat upon by either of them.

"Go ahead and sit down, Laura," Steffie urged as she squeezed by her to answer a question Rory was asking about the computer.

Laura swallowed against a suddenly dry throat. Surely there had to be another chair? Or a stool. Or even a crate.

But she found nothing in the cluttered little office that she could possibly sit on. Not even floor space. "Maybe we should wait for Fletcher," she suggested. "I'm sure he'll be here soon. He wouldn't want to miss the show."

"He can watch it later," B.J. replied in her gruff, decisive voice. "We made copies of the CD for everyone. Besides, most of the photos were taken before he moved in."

Laura reluctantly digested this information, thought about the prospect of actually *sitting on Cort Dimitri's lap* and considered claiming that she preferred to stand. It *had* been a long flight. Her legs *were* somewhat cramped from sitting.

But if she were to say so, others might take her refusal to sit on his lap as a sign that she was holding a grudge against him. Or, worse yet, that she was *afraid* to sit on his lap. Afraid of the prolonged, undeniably intimate contact.

Cort's gaze lingered on her face. Beyond his pleasant nonchalance glimmered a disturbing awareness. He knew of her reluctance to sit on his lap. His gaze penetrated hers, as if searching for the reason.

"Here," he said, rising slowly without breaking eye contact. "Take the chair. I'd just as soon—"

"No, no, don't be silly!" Mortified for causing the awkwardness she'd sworn to avoid, Laura caught his shoulders before he'd fully risen and pressed him back down, her smile desperately friendly. "There's no need for you to stand, Cort." She hastily withdrew her hands from his wide, solid shoulders, conscious of the thrill coursing up her arms from the brawny hardness of him. Heat lingered in her face, and she was aware that the others had cast casual glances their way. "I don't mind sitting on your lap," Laura assured him. At a sudden thought, she added, "Oh! Unless *you* would mind. Or if Steffie would rather sit here."

"No, no, I'll clear off a space at my desk and perch there," Steffie announced, appearing beside her. "Park yourself, girlfriend." Grabbing Laura by the arms, she pushed her down, down, down onto Cort's warm, hard lap. "You don't mind," Stef asked him. "Do you, Cort?"

"Not at all."

The polite utterance rushed against Laura's jaw with the fragrance of fine brandy. His suddenly overwhelming nearness sent frissons of sensation racing across her skin, beneath her sweater, front and back. But most distracting was the heat radiating through her from the contact with his sinewy thighs.

Forcing herself to breathe evenly, she directed her gaze toward the television screen and concentrated fiercely on controlling her heart rate.

Nonchalance. She had to strive for friendly nonchalance.

But seated as she was—diagonally across his lap—she couldn't help but see his dark, rugged face only inches from hers. He seemed to be studying her.

His gaze slowly swept over her hair. Her face. Her mouth.

Irrational heat shimmered through her, and she nearly groaned. He was only *looking,* for God's sake! And yet she *felt* his gaze, like a feather-light caress. Like a shot of potent brandy, warming her all the way through.

The lights clicked off, cloaking them in yet a deeper feeling of intimacy. Rory's rock music blared from the speakers and colors flashed across the screen.

Cort shifted his large, solid body in the chair, leaning Laura into a more comfortable position against his tautly muscled chest and shoulder.

She resisted. She didn't *want* a more comfortable position. She was already far too aware of every muscle he moved, every breath he took. Of his strong, steady heartbeat. His body heat engulfing her like a warm bath. The musky, masculine fragrance of that heat, so instrinsically familiar.

She had to calm down! She remained rigid and tense, not allowing her back to rest against him.

The show, she realized, had already begun. A slide show. She'd somehow missed the opening.

A photo of the Hays Street house—the shabby, threadbare Victorian manor where they'd all lived—finally distracted her enough to engage her attention. She'd loved that house. She'd been happy there. At least, for a while.

Next came a smiling group photo of them on the front porch. The Hays Street gang, in all their youthful splendor.

Rory had added comments to the computerized slide show in a dramatic voice-over. "The start of a new era, my friends. The Year of the Cat." The photo showed Mangy, the tabby stray they'd adopted as their own. The next showed Steffie in a sexy Halloween costume, dressed as a cat.

Rory had recorded a long, suggestive *"Mee-ee-ooww!"*

Everyone laughed. Cort, Laura noticed from the corner of her eye, smiled.

Photos flashed by of their first Halloween party, when they'd decorated the place as a haunted house with so much zest that neighbors stopped in to take pictures of it. Someone had persuaded a husky, muscle-bound Hoss to dress up in a huge diaper and baby bonnet for the party. He'd regretted it and sulked in a corner.

"Blackmail material, Coach," Cort remarked, his voice low and wry and very close to Laura's ear.

Tamika let out a delighted squeal from beside them. "Wouldn't the team get a kick out of that?"

The next photo showed Christmastime, when Laura had badgered them all into stringing popcorn around a scraggly tree. Rory had supplied them with microwave buttered popcorn, though, which kept slipping out of their fingers.

"Hey, you can never have enough butter, I always says," said Rory.

Laura smiled while the others volleyed teasing comments and shared hilarious anecdotes about every photo displayed: Tamika teaching B.J. how to dance; Rory catching on fire while grilling hamburgers; Cort smirking as he doused him with a garden hose.

And then came a photo that made Laura's smile wobble and her heart lurch. It was a close-up of Cort and her, entwined in an embrace on the sofa, deeply involved in a kiss. His dark, large hand was splayed at the small of her back, the other entangled in her hair. Their eyes were closed and their faces flushed with passion.

"And here we have Cort and Laura once again proving the superlative bestowed upon them by lower and upper classmen alike, 'The Couple Most Likely To.'" Rory paused in his droll commentary for an audible "Whew!," as if he were shaking off a sweat. "Someone stop 'em. Where's that garden hose when you really need it?"

Chuckles, groans and protests rose in a chorus around her, but Laura sat in stricken silence, struggling to draw a breath past her thundering heart, which seemed to have lodged in her throat.

The screen changed to Tamika and Hoss dressed up for a dance, Steffie caught in an old nightshirt with rollers in her hair, Rory and his band rehearsing in the unfurnished dining room.

But Laura could no longer focus on the slide show. The sight of herself in Cort's arms had reminded her too vividly of what had gone on between them...and of the deep, chaotic feelings he hadn't reciprocated.

He, too, seemed suddenly subdued. Although he'd been relaxed and uttering dry witticisms that sent the others into whoops of laughter, he'd since fallen silent, his body still, his muscles clenched.

She didn't dare look at him. She couldn't bear it. How could she possibly sit through even one more photo of them together?

"And that, my friends," Rory announced, "brings us to the action segment of our presentation."

With a dramatic drumroll, the still photographs gave way to the lifelike sound and action of videotape.

2

CORT REALIZED IMMEDIATELY that he'd made a mistake by having Laura sit on his lap. He hadn't actually thought she'd do it. He'd read the reluctance in her gaze and had expected her to decline. She'd taken him completely by surprise when she'd refused the chair he'd offered, smiled her friendliest smile, pushed him back down and insisted she didn't mind sitting on him.

She'd lied.

She minded. She sat as stiff and still as an icicle, and her glance hadn't once strayed his way. If she could have hovered above him to avoid all contact, he believed she would. Why, then, was she sitting on his lap when she obviously didn't want to?

More importantly, *why didn't she want to?* Because she couldn't forgive his cold, hasty goodbye? Because her illusions about him had long ago fled, and she now saw him as he really was? Or simply because the years had turned them into strangers?

Ridiculous for him to wonder. He hadn't expected a warm reception from her. Hadn't really hoped for one. He could have handled a snub much easier. At least he would have understood a snub.

This, however, made no sense at all. She was forcing herself to sit on his lap. Was this her version of an olive branch—a declaration of forgiveness? A public show of her acceptance of him? A valiant effort to please Steffie?

Whatever her reasoning, the situation was awkward, tense and disturbing. Worse than that, actually. It was hell.

The hell had begun the moment her firm, rounded bottom had settled snugly against his thighs. As much as she'd changed, she still fit too nicely there. Still felt too damn good.

His blood warmed and coursed harder through his veins.

She looked different than he remembered, yes, but not different enough to give him the mental distance he suddenly needed. Her face, though slightly thinner, was the same one he'd gazed into day after day, night after night, while he'd made love to her.

From this close range, he could easily see that her light, golden skin was every bit as smooth as it had been years ago, when he'd been free to touch her. Free to slide his hands beneath her clothes and savor her voluptuous warmth and velvet softness.

With a deep, silent intake of breath, he forced his attention away from her skin...and her sweater, and all the intimate territory that had once been his to explore. Territory that was now as distant and mysterious to him as the moon.

He tried to direct his attention to the television screen, which displayed comical snapshots, but soon found himself distracted by Laura's hair. She wore it bound at her nape with a scarf. He'd been disappointed by its darker, more subdued shade of blond when he'd first seen her. But from where he sat now, every strand shone like sunlit honey, with a silky luster that made him long to free the shining mass and thrust his fingers into its fragrant heaviness.

He had to curl his hand into a fist to resist touching it.

Her scent struck a familiar chord, too. Not the light,

flowery fragrance she wore, but the elusive, personal aroma that somehow rose from the very essence of her. It reminded him of apple pie, hot and sweet, with just the right hint of spice and tartness to make his mouth water.

Mmm.

Which brought to mind the taste of her.

A jolt of heat went through him and he forced his unseeing gaze to the television. He couldn't think about the taste of her now—her mouth, her skin, her delectable body— not when his arousal strained behind his zipper, only inches away from her curvaceous hip. How easy it would be to wrap his hand around her outer hip and pull her firmly against him.

He fought against a hot, red haze and finally focused on the television. He'd become spoiled, he realized. His financial success had assured him of having whatever he wanted, whenever he wanted. Women included. This would have to be an exception. He couldn't have Laura. Couldn't touch her.

Shouldn't even be thinking about her.

The photos flashed by on the screen, and the joking comments of the others helped to distract him somewhat. He even managed a few dry quips of his own.

But then came the snapshot of Laura and him caught in a deep, hungry kiss. And the desire kindled again in his loins, hot and insistent.

God, he'd loved kissing her. Never before or since had a woman enslaved him so completely with a simple kiss. Never before or since had he wanted anyone as he'd wanted her. They'd made love every day, every night; whenever they'd found the chance. And still, he hadn't been able to get enough of her. He'd been obsessed. He knew that now. A dangerous thing, that kind of sexual obsession.

She didn't know, of course, the effort it had cost him to break away from her. Or that even now, fifteen years later, random thoughts of her filtered through his mind whenever he became aroused. A damn nuisance at times.

Not so bad at others...

The photo of their kiss, he realized, had seemed to bother her, too. The soft smile that had been playing across her full, smooth lips had fled, and Cort sensed the tension within her coiling even tighter.

He remembered surefire ways to ease that tension. Of course, he'd have to wind it *much* tighter before he'd allow her any release.

He could start right here, at her tender nape, beneath the tie of her scarf, where wispy tendrils danced with his every breath. He would press his mouth there—swirl his tongue just beneath her hairline, then around to her ear, until a groan caught in her throat...and her back arched... and her hips moved against him....

Thankfully, Rory's announcement interrupted the heated flow of Cort's imagination. He couldn't take much more.

Rory had said something about the action segment of their production. Before Cort could entirely divorce himself from the seductive images in his head, a very different set of images moved and laughed on the screen.

Video. Lifelike action, color and sound. Snatches of life in the Hays Street house—rollicking parties, sleepy Sunday mornings and surprise attacks on the unsuspecting, catching each of them in embarrassingly candid situations and conversations.

Interspersed throughout this "slice of life" were shots of Laura and him. Kissing, usually. Or running their hands over each other in long, scintillating paths. Gazing with passionate absorption into each other's eyes. Slow-dancing at a party in some private corner, moving together in blatantly sexual synchrony.

A muffled sound rose from Laura's throat, and she shifted forward to rise from his lap.

Cort acted without thinking. He caught her to stop her from leaving. He sensed her distress, and wanted to comfort. To soothe. To hold.

He gripped her hip and thigh, and anchored her to his lap.

Her gaze swung to his, her eyes wide with surprise. And reproach. And something he couldn't quite read. They glimmered the color of sweet, hot cocoa—the exact shade he remembered from the first time he'd undressed her. Color blazed in her skin, matching the warmth that simmered in his.

His attention dipped to her mouth. *Her delectable mouth...*

"Let me go," she said in a tremulous whisper.

He did. Immediately.

LAURA HEADED BLINDLY toward the back of the house, barely noting the rooms through which she passed, needing to find a place where she could be alone. She veered through the first escape hatch she saw—sliding glass doors that led to an outside deck. Heedless of the cold and the tiny snowflakes drifting around her, she leaned against the side railing and stared up at the murky night sky.

She needed a few moments alone to collect herself. A few moments would do it, she was sure. She breathed in deeply of the frosty mountain air, letting it cool her. It would take a good deal of cooling to bring her temperature into line. She felt flushed with heat. From embarrassment, mostly. And anger.

Yes, embarrassment and anger.

She'd wanted to leave the room immediately when the video segment had begun. But for some unfathomable reason, she couldn't tear her eyes from the screen. A form of self-punishment, she supposed.

How humiliating it had been to see herself so obviously infatuated, so wretchedly besotted, with a man who hadn't really cared in the least about her. He'd simply taken what she'd been so happy to give. He probably could have made love to her right then and there, in front of their whole group of pals—with the camera rolling—and she wouldn't have noticed anyone but him.

What a damn fool she'd been.

The humiliation of watching herself with Cort on the screen had been bad enough, but when the pressure in her chest had grown too great and she'd attempted to leave, he'd had the unmitigated gall to stop her. The very idea filled her with rage.

What made him think he had the right to touch her in any way, let alone to detain her against her will? Why in heaven's name had he wanted to? To prove that he could? To show that he still had the power to melt away her common sense?

Never had she been more enraged at a person in her life. Not even when he'd said those hateful things before he'd left her. She hadn't been angry at all back then. Only hurt. Grievously hurt.

But she was indeed angry now. At him. Entirely at him.

Filling her lungs with the much-needed coolness, she stared out through the falling snow and concentrated on calming herself. Once the initial surge of anger had abated, she admitted that maybe some of the anger—a very small portion—might have been directed at her.

And that maybe not all of the heat had been due to anger, or even embarrassment.

As vexing as the truth was, she had to face it. She'd been ensnared once again by his nearness. His gaze. His silent but palpable interest in her. She'd felt the heat gathering in him, the rhythm of his heart quicken, and she'd responded. Oh, not in a way that anyone else could detect. Only with a secret warming of her blood and rushing of her heart.

Worst of all, when his strong hands had gripped her hip and thigh and pressed her down onto his lap, her pulse had leaped with a fierce, sudden longing. She'd wanted to stay in the controlling grip of those hands. To turn herself around on his lap, move against his muscle-hard body, revel in the erotic pleasure of his enticing heat.

She gulped in another huge lungful of air and raked her trembling fingers through her bangs. Good Lord, she'd put *that* kind of nonsense behind her long ago. Erotic pleasure. Enticing heat. Who needed any of it?

Shaken by feelings she'd almost forgotten existed, she struggled to put it all in perspective. She'd simply been influenced by the nostalgia. Rory and B.J.'s photos had carried her back to a crazy, passionate time in her youth, and she'd responded to the memories—*not* to the man himself. That was an important distinction. She had grown far, far beyond her teenage infatuation with Cort Dimitri.

A chill finally pervaded her bulky sweater, and she wrapped her arms around herself to retain some body heat.

She heard the quiet *whirrr* of the glass door sliding open behind her, and bit her lip in dismay. She really did need a few more moments alone to collect herself. Turning around to reluctantly greet whoever had joined her, she felt her dismay drastically deepen. Her heart paused.

Cort Dimitri stepped out onto the dimly lit deck and closed the door behind him.

Like her, he wore no coat—only an expensive forest-green sweater that stretched neatly across his broad shoulders, and a pair of gray gabardine trousers that reminded her of the long, lean, muscular thighs she'd been sitting on so recently. A few snowflakes caught and glittered on his ebony hair and lashes, while his midnight-blue gaze pinned her against the railing.

"Laura, I'm sorry." His deep, quiet voice filled the night. "I was out of line when I tried to stop you from leaving." The sincerity on his dark, arresting face kept her still and breathless. One end of his mouth turned up in a slight, wry smile. "I don't know what I was thinking."

Something about the soft gruffness and hint of irony in his last statement suffused her with warmth.

Damn him! Damn him for gazing at her with that intensity, and for daring to corner her alone, and for having the decency to apologize. As much as she wished it weren't so, she knew his apology was sincere, and found that she couldn't quite hold on to her anger. Couldn't he have left her at least her anger?

She did, of course, have her pride. "Forget it." She lifted a negligent shoulder. "You surprised me, that's all." Leveling him a meaningful stare, she added, "Just don't let it happen again."

He held her stare, looking rather surprised himself. Squinting at her through the snow, he pursed his lips and studied her. "Don't let *what* happen again?"

"Don't..." Laura swallowed against a sudden fluttering in her throat. *Don't touch me, or hold me, or make my heart pound.* "...manhandle me."

Again, she'd clearly surprised him. He gave a small, rueful smile that didn't quite reach his eyes. "You've changed."

Yes, she had. In many ways. But she knew exactly which

change he referred to. At one time, she wouldn't have stopped him from touching her or holding her in any way. She wouldn't have been opposed to his *manhandling*. "I'm glad you've noticed."

Thrusting his hands into the deep pockets of his trousers, he sauntered across the deck and leaned against the railing beside her. She wanted to move away, unreasonably daunted by his nearness. Pride kept her staunchly in place. She refused to be intimidated...or affected in any way, for that matter.

His gaze lingered on her face, filling her again with annoying warmth. He then looked out into the snowy night, where majestic mountains loomed in the distant blackness. "I guess I just wanted to make sure I'd get the chance to talk to you before you...rushed off somewhere."

She raised an eyebrow at that. He'd changed, too, if he wanted to *talk*. "What did you want to talk to me about?"

His gaze remained fixed on some distant point. "I gathered you were embarrassed by the photos."

She stiffened, unsure of how to respond. Unsure of how he would interpret any answer she might give. Faintly, she asked, "Embarrassed? Why should I be embarrassed?"

As softly as the smattering of snowflakes pelting against their faces, he replied, "Maybe because we made damn fools of ourselves every chance we got?"

"Oh. *That*."

He slanted her a glance that sparkled. "Yes, *that*."

She wondered if he knew how much he'd surprised her. Could he possibly be as embarrassed as she was by their past behavior? She didn't see why he should be. He hadn't been the one suffering from delusions of love-ever-after. He hadn't been the one left behind, looking like a naive ninny.

"I behaved pretty much like a sex-crazed idiot," he re-marked, "didn't I?"

She was, for some reason, beginning to feel vindicated. "Pretty much."

"And I...took full advantage of your...innocence."

Memories evoked by those words throbbed almost painfully in her chest. "If you hadn't, someone else would have, I'm sure." A lie. No other man had ever intoxicated her with passion as Cort had. She wouldn't have lost her head in quite the same way with anyone else. But she saw no reason for him to know it.

He shifted to search her face, a frown in his eyes, as if he sensed she hid some truth from him. His efforts seemed only to frustrate him. "I owe you another apology," he said at last. "I shouldn't have said what I did when I left. You didn't deserve my harshness. And crudeness. I'm sorry."

She gaped at him. Never had she expected this particu-lar apology. She struggled for a moment to find her voice. "No, don't be sorry. You only told me the truth. If it was harsh, well..." she shrugged, realizing as she spoke that she believed what she was saying "...at least you forced me to face the facts."

Which had been the hardest thing she had ever done.

Love? he'd scoffed as he'd packed his bags. *I don't love you, Laura. I want you. There's a big difference. This is the only "real" thing we've ever had between us....* And he'd put her hand on his zipper, against the hardness swelling there.

Grappling to hide the pain that memory still inflicted, she went on in a soft, soothing tone, "In fact, I believe I owe you my thanks. You taught me a valuable lesson."

"I was a son of a bitch, and you know it. I wouldn't blame you if you never—"

"No, I mean it, Cort. You really did teach me an important lesson. Do you remember how dead set I was on telling my parents to go to hell when they insisted that I break up with you?"

He fell silent, his attention caught. Slowly, he nodded.

"I was ready to give up all their financial support and pay my own way, even if it meant dropping out of college."

Again he nodded, almost warily, as if expecting a vengeful punch line.

"How could I have been so crazy? I was willing to throw my future away, and for what? Love!" She mimicked the exact tone he'd used with her, all those years ago. "I know better now, of course. Thanks to your honesty. You could have told me some pretty lie, and I would have mourned for our 'ill-fated love.' Instead, I had to face reality, and I learned from my mistakes. I've learned never to base important decisions on...on whimsy." She gazed deeply into his eyes, which had grown unreadable. "So I do thank you. You didn't hurt me in any lasting way. You actually helped me." Although she meant every word, these last few stuck in her throat, and she had to force them out. "And time did prove you right. There wasn't anything between us except sex."

Something flashed within the midnight depths of his eyes, then faded away, leaving them somehow even darker than before. His mouth hardened. His jaw squared. But his voice, when he spoke, was soft. Dangerously so. "Does that mean you forgive me?"

An odd reluctance delayed her reply. She had no doubt that he regretted his harsh way of breaking off their affair, and she'd already told him that he hadn't hurt her in any lasting way. Why, then, did she sense some hidden challenge in his gaze. "Yes, of course I forgive you," she said at last.

They stared at each other for a dozen or more heartbeats.

He then slipped his hands around her waist and pulled her slowly, determinedly, into a hug. "Thank you, Laura Merritt," he breathed into her hair, "for your forgiveness."

"And thank *you* for your apology," she replied in a breathless whisper against his shoulder, once again aware of his strength, his muscled hardness, the achingly familiar scent of his hair and skin.

"You're shivering." He drew her deeper into his arms, shielding her from the chill; pressing her body against his to share his heat.

"We should go inside," she croaked, feeling very strongly that she should, even as she savored the easy authority of his embrace; the scrape of his beard-stubbled jaw against her temple; the seductive rhythm of his heart that brought to mind so many sensuous escapades.

He drew back just far enough to peer down at her. Slanting his face into intimate alignment with hers, he rasped, "I have a better way to stay warm." Slowly he lowered his head and brushed his mouth across the length of hers. A feather-light stroke. Velvety soft. From one corner to the other.

Her breath caught, trapped in her lungs by a sudden welling of desire. Heat tingled across her lips and sizzled through her bloodstream. She couldn't turn away from him. Couldn't force out a single word.

When he lifted his head, a compelling heat blazed from his eyes. She stared at him in dazed astonishment that he would do such a thing. That she would let him. That the pleasure had been so incredibly intense.

A groan rose in his throat. He closed his eyes and took her mouth in a deep, moving kiss.

Desire flared between them, hot and swift. She gave herself over to it, reveling in its fierceness, and in the rich, arousing taste of his mouth...a taste she'd hungered for in the most secret of her dreams. His strong, commanding hands swept along the curve of her face and held her steady while he angled his kiss and thrust his tongue in a bold, intimate invasion.

She wanted to capture him there. Hold him inside. Feast on the heat, the thrill, the intoxicating passion.

The very intensity of her desire tripped some internal alarm, and sanity rushed back with dizzying speed. What was she doing? Had she completely lost her mind? Yes, she had!

With a moan of dismay, she pulled free of his kiss, her heart slamming against her rib cage.

He stared at her with a stunned expression on his harshly beautiful face, as if she'd slapped him awake from a pleasurable dream.

"Why did you *do* that?" she whispered frantically between erratic breaths.

His breathing sounded as labored as hers. His eyes burned bright. His voice emerged low and hoarse. "For the same reason you didn't stop me."

His reply shook her almost as much as the kiss. She couldn't deny that he'd given her a sporting chance to refuse. He'd swept his mouth along hers, then waited for her reaction. She'd virtually begged him with her silence to keep on.

"Tell me, Laura," he commanded gruffly, drawing near her again, his gaze roaming in seductive paths across her face, "why didn't you stop me?"

Desire rose sharply within her, and she swallowed a gasp of alarm. "Curiosity. Just...curiosity." She backed away from him and strove to reclaim her dignity. "And I can assure you, it's been satisfied."

Her back hit the sliding glass door.

He planted a hand against the door frame beside her head. "I don't believe curiosity had much to do with it," he whispered, his breath warm and fragrant against her mouth. "And don't try to tell me you're satisfied."

She stared wordlessly at him, mesmerized by the intensity simmering in his midnight gaze; her heart pounding in her throat.

He removed his hand and straightened his stance, granting her access to the door.

She whirled away, slid open the door and strode inside. Summoning all her self-control, she waited until she had rounded the first corner, safely out of his sight, before she broke into a run.

She'd been wrong. She hadn't grown beyond the foolishness of her youth, and she couldn't trust herself alone with Cort Dimitri. He still ignited a dangerous flame within her—a flame that could easily burn away the stability she so badly needed.

This, then, was the ultimate reason that fate had thrust him back into her life at this particular time. To remind her of the danger that lay in wait for her if she should stray from the path she'd chosen. Her temporary relapse into mindless passion had frightened every last doubt out of her.

She would go through with the plans she'd made with Fletcher. She'd take refuge in their rational approach to life and love and family. She'd be strong in her platonic alliance with him—and she'd avoid the temptation of Cort Dimitri *at all costs*.

As she drew nearer to the babble of conversation at the front of the house, she almost cried out loud in relief. Fletcher had arrived! He was here, bringing with him the clear, steady light of reason. The mere sound of his pleasantly pragmatic voice reminded her of who she'd become, and who she strove to be—a well-established career woman; a loyal and steadfast friend; most important of all, a mother.

A mother!

Passion meant nothing in the face of such goals.

Sweet, clear reason had returned. She was safe.

"FLETCHER, YOU REMEMBER my brother, Cort, don't you?" Steffie flashed her usual buoyant smile at them both. "I know he moved out shortly after you moved in to the Hays Street house, but—"

"Of course I remember Cort. He whipped me good in a game of chess. I've been hoping for a rematch someday."

Cort answered with an obligatory smile and handshake. The guy's grip was firm, his gaze intelligent. He looked pretty much the same as he had back in their Hays Street days—average height, slender build; short brown hair with a well-trimmed beard; a nondescript face; fashionable, wire-rimmed glasses. He wore a buttoned-down white collar beneath a navy sweater, neatly pressed jeans and high sneakers.

There was nothing immediately obvious to dislike about the guy. That didn't stop Cort from keenly assessing him. He couldn't forget Fletcher's quiet interest in Laura, which he probably thought no one had noticed.

What, exactly, was the nature of their relationship now? Steffie had told him it was strictly platonic, and that he and Laura worked closely together in the course of business. Cort had seen nothing to suggest it was anything more. Since he'd unobtrusively joined the group a short while ago, he'd watched Fletcher cheerfully socializing with everyone present, paying no special attention to Laura. But they *had* shared amiable glances, finished each other's sentences and included each other's names in casual conversation.

Nothing extraordinary about that. They were, after all, longtime friends and business associates.

No reason Cort should want to choke him.

Cort exchanged a few polite words with Fletcher, joked with B.J. about the new black rose tattoo on her forearm and nodded his appreciation to Rory as he switched from the blaring electric guitar to the quieter acoustic one. While everyone else applauded Rory's choice of guitars and songs, Cort leaned against the fireplace mantel and nursed his brandy.

Laura, meanwhile, joined the cluster of friends around Fletcher. She pretended not to notice as Cort stared at her. She did notice, though. A rosy hue flooded her face and she developed an avid interest in everything being said.

Cort cursed himself for being a fool. He hadn't meant to kiss her. He'd wanted only to apologize. What the hell had come over him? The apology itself had gone better than he'd hoped. She'd actually thanked him for it...and for his "honesty" when he'd left her.

Honesty. He'd been deliberately crude. And cruel.

And she, God love her, had forgiven him. Absolved him of all wrongdoing. *Time proved you right,* she'd said. *There wasn't anything between us except sex.*

His muscles had clenched as if he'd been sucker punched. He hadn't expected that from her. She'd always been so starry-eyed. Idealistic. Passionately, blindly in love with him.

A mocking voice laughed from somewhere deep inside him. *You didn't think she'd really fallen for a hood like you, did you? Of course she came to her senses. You knew she would.* Yes, he had known she would. He just hadn't realized how much of an impact her new clear-sightedness would have on him.

And he hadn't known, until he'd kissed her, how damn much he still wanted her.

"Fletcher," she was saying in that soft, affectionate way of hers that made a man feel sure he would always be the center of her universe, "you've got to come see Hoss and Tamika's baby. He's asleep upstairs. You don't mind, do you, Tam?"

Tamika waved her blessing. Laura caught hold of Fletcher's arm and urged him up the stairs.

Cort drank deeply of his brandy and waited for them to come back down. He knew they were going up to see the baby, but the sight of them climbing the stairs together twisted something in his gut. He remembered the times *he'd* climbed the stairs with her, leaving everyone else behind. They'd never reappeared until morning, or until circumstances demanded it.

The smartest thing he could do, Cort realized, trying not to glare at the empty stairway, was to call his answering service for messages, invent some crisis that needed his immediate attention and get the hell out of here.

But even as he thought it, he knew he wouldn't. Because he never had been one to give up on anything he wanted without a damn good reason. She'd run from him tonight. Twice. First because he'd held her, and then because he'd kissed her. She couldn't have made it more obvious that she didn't want him.

Or…that she didn't *want* to want him. He couldn't forget the way she'd responded to his kiss—as if she were still passionately, blindly in love with him.

No, he wouldn't delude himself into believing she was, or that she ever really had been. But neither would he turn his back on the possibilities raised by the combustible chemistry between them. If sex was all they'd ever had, so be it. He could live with that. He could definitely liven up his holidays with that.

He would, he decided, stay. And satisfy his own "curiosity." He'd discover just how many things about her—about *them*—hadn't changed at all.

One thing had. He could afford her now.

"Hey, Cort, I believe I saw a big-screen TV downstairs," Hoss remarked, strolling over to stand beside him with a beer. "Bet we can catch the last quarter of the Georgia Tech game. How 'bout it?"

Cort welcomed the distraction. Rory set his guitar aside and followed them to the rec room, where they watched football, smoked cigars and shot a game of pool. B.J. soon joined them, and eventually, Fletcher did, too.

After the game, they all returned to the great room where Laura, Steffie and Tamika sat on the sofa, engrossed in quiet conversation. Cort had barely reached his favorite spot beside the fireplace when a shriek drew every gaze to Steffie.

"You're going to *what*?" Steffie cried, leaping up from the sofa and staring at Laura with wide, incredulous eyes. Tamika also gaped at Laura, openmouthed.

Laura's face, Cort noticed, turned a deep shade of red as her gaze shot beyond Steffie and Tamika to the others who were now listening. She put a finger to her lips to shush Steffie, but she was obviously beyond the shushing point.

"A baby?" Steffie screeched. "You're going to have a *baby? With Fletcher?*"

WHY, OH WHY, had she opened her mouth about her plans? Laura could have kicked herself. But seeing her little godson sleeping so sweetly upstairs and knowing that she could have a baby of her own by this time next year had suddenly seemed so overwhelmingly exciting that she hadn't been able to keep from confiding in her two best friends.

She hadn't realized the others had returned to the great room, or that Steffie would shriek out the news.

Everyone now gaped at her, dumbfounded. Even Fletcher looked surprised, but only because he hadn't expected to share their plans just yet. He met her troubled gaze, and with a nervous but touchingly proud smile, he moved closer to her in a show of support.

"I don't understand," Tamika said, breaking the stunned silence. "Have you been dating Fletcher? When the hell did *that* start? You call me every week, and never said a word about it."

"How could you and Fletcher be having a baby?" Steffie's glossy dark hair swung around her piquant face as she shook her head in bewilderment.

"Are you telling me that *he* got you *pregnant?*" B.J. demanded in disbelief, her auburn eyebrows shooting up her pale forehead until they merged with her buzz cut.

"Wow. A baby," mused Rory. "You and old Fletch. Cool."

"He knocked you up?" Hoss pressed forward with his mighty shoulders squared, his glare at Fletcher a blatant threat. "What's he gonna do about it?"

"No, no, wait." Laura stood up from the sofa and lifted her arms in a calming gesture as Fletcher shifted closer to her. "I guess I'd better explain."

She cast a self-conscious glance around the room and became intensely aware of the one person who hadn't spoken; the one she refused to look directly in the eye. Cort stood with his broad shoulder jammed against the mantel and a brandy snifter clutched in his hand. That hand had frozen halfway to his mouth, his fingers curled in a fist around the delicate stem of his glass.

"Fletcher has agreed to father my baby," Laura clarified, speaking to the group at large, "but I'm not pregnant yet. We've set an appointment to start trying next week."

B.J. choked and spewed beer out of her nose. Steffie's jaw dropped. Tamika frowned.

Glass shattered near the fireplace. Cort stood with only the bowl of the snifter in his hand. The stem, it seemed, had cracked. The hearth below glinted with shards and jagged pieces of the snifter's base.

He didn't spare it a glance.

Laura wouldn't meet his gaze, but she felt it. His concentrated attention made her skin heat up and her stomach churn. She wished he wasn't here. Cort and his stirring gazes and drugging kisses had no place in her life—the safe, solid life she'd built for herself and her future baby. The sooner she could put her plan into action, the better.

"You've *set an appointment* to start trying?" Hoss's wide forehead crinkled in bewilderment. "If you need an appointment, sugar, I can't see this relationship working out."

"I still don't understand," Tamika loudly complained. "Are you and Fletcher in love? Are you getting married?"

"A baby," Rory repeated. "You and old Fletch. Who would have thought it?"

"Why's everyone so darned surprised?" Fletcher grumbled. "I'll make a good dad. I coach kids' baseball every summer."

"But I thought you two were just friends," Tamika said.

"We are," Laura confirmed.

"I mean, *platonic* friends," Tamika specified.

"Exactly."

"Then how—?"

"Oh!" Laura felt her face flush with embarrassment as she realized where much of their confusion lay. "We intend to do it by artificial means." At the continued blank looks, she expounded, "You know, scientifically. At a clinic."

"Not that it's anyone's business," Fletcher muttered.

"Would anyone like another drink?" Steffie inquired a little too brightly as she took the broken brandy glass from Cort's hand and nudged the shattered pieces from the hearth into the fireplace with her foot. "Or two? Or three?"

"Mercy sakes alive!" Tamika planted her hands on her hips. "Isn't artificial insemination expensive?"

"A little," Laura admitted, "but—"

"Then why do artificial insemination?" A puzzled frown knit Rory's blond eyebrows. "Save the cash, man. If you guys are sure you want a kid, just go upstairs and—"

"Why don't you shut up and play that damn guitar of yours?" Cort suggested to him quietly, ready to strangle Rory with his own ponytail if he finished verbalizing that thought.

"Fletcher's right," Laura proclaimed. "It's no one's business how we choose to accomplish our objectives. I shouldn't have even told you." She glared at every face—except Cort's, which she avoided entirely. "I don't want to hear any more discussion about that aspect of our plan."

Only when everyone looked sufficiently abashed did her expression mellow. "Think instead about the end result. A baby! Don't you see how perfect this will be? Fletcher and I have been friends for fifteen years. We know, really know, how the other thinks and feels about the important issues of life. We'll be giving our son or daughter a sturdy base that won't be ripped apart by emotional upheaval or divorce."

"Oh, God," Steffie groaned, burying her face in her hand. "I should have known you'd resort to something like this."

"I'm going to ask one more time before I start busting heads," Tamika warned. "Are you two getting married, or not?"

"No! That's the beauty of it. Our parenting alliance will be based on mutual respect, not...whimsy." Laura's color deepened, and she added, "Or, worse, sex."

An invisible hand tightened around Cort's throat. She hadn't as much as glanced his way, but he felt as if she'd pointed at him as an example of a past sexual disaster. She'd used the word *whimsy* earlier to describe the lesson she'd learned from him.

Was *he* to blame for this? Had his callous dismissal of their affair set her against sexual relationships altogether? Had her disillusionment at such a young age turned her to science to father her child—*and to Fletcher?* The hand around Cort's throat squeezed with a vengeance.

"We'll go on living the way we have been." She settled down onto the sofa and Fletcher sat beside her. "Friends and partners. We'll share custody and live within walking distance of each other, as we do right now. And we'll bring up our child in the faith we both happen to share. What can be more perfect?"

"A happy marriage?" suggested Steffie.

"Oh, come on, Stef," Laura admonished softly. "You know how rare an animal *that* is."

Steffie flushed, unable to argue. She had, after all, just come through a divorce herself.

"All of us know how painful it can be for a child growing up in a broken home," Laura said, "or with parents so resentful of each other that they spend all their time trying to spite the other."

No one could deny that she had a point. They'd all come from families whose relationships were less than blissful. Their lack of satisfying family ties had been the common denominator that had drawn them together in the first place.

"Well, call me old-fashioned, but I believe in love and marriage," Tamika declared, "and having children in wedlock."

"Of course you do," Laura replied patiently. "You're one of the rare, lucky few who are happily married. But that's only because you've known Hoss for so long. You've developed a good, strong friendship over the years, just like mine and Fletcher's."

"It's *not* like yours and Fletcher's," argued Tamika.

"It is! Well, minus the sex. Which, in the grand scheme of things, is really a minor detail."

"Minor detail!" Hoss turned an outraged frown to Tamika. "Did she say 'minor detail'?"

"Calm down, Hoss." His wife patted his arm with an affectionate smirk. "She didn't mean it as a slur against you."

"Minor detail," he muttered. He narrowed his eyes at Laura. "Who the hell have you been sleeping with, girl?"

"No one, I'll bet," Steffie retorted.

"Steffie!" Laura stared at her in reproach, clearly embarrassed.

"It's true, isn't it? When was the last time you had a real relationship with a man?"

Laura rose from the sofa with her lips compressed and an angry, wounded expression in her eyes. "I can't believe this." Her soft voice shook as she looked around the room. "I expected you, our best friends, to be happy about our news. To share in our joy of starting a family. But no. Here you are, acting like a bunch of high school kids, focusing on...on sex!"

"Or lack thereof," B.J. quipped dryly.

"Oh, Laur, I'm so sorry!" Steffie's eyes shone with contrition as she enfolded Laura in a hug. "Of course I'm happy for you. We're *all* happy for you. You'll make a wonderful mother, and Fletcher will be a great dad. And we all want to be good aunts and uncles."

"We're just worried about this...this sudden decision," Tamika gently added.

"It's a crazy, harebrained scheme," Hoss insisted. "Sex ain't no minor detail."

Laura drew away from Steffie and rounded on Hoss. "Sex is entirely beside the point!"

"She's right."

Cort's quiet proclamation plunged the room into stunned silence—maybe because no one had expected him to contribute to the conversation...or to take that particular stand.

He leveled a cool stare at Laura, whom he'd surprised into actually looking at him. "Sex *is* beside the point," he agreed, strolling from the fireplace to join the group, "unless it causes a problem in your relationship some time down the road."

"It won't," Laura quietly swore.

As Cort advanced, she sat down again on the sofa beside Fletcher, as if she needed his nearness for moral support.

Cort fought to suppress a scowl. Why the hell had she chosen *Fletcher* to play such a pivotal role? *The father of her baby.* The very idea filled Cort with aversion. He knew what that role would mean to Laura. She'd be bound to him in an utterly profound way for the rest of her life.

He lowered himself into an armchair directly across from them. "If you don't mind, I'd like to play the devil's advocate for a moment." No one voiced an objection. "What will happen if—or rather, *when*—either of you becomes involved with someone else? Don't you think that might create the exact kind of emotional turmoil you're trying to avoid?"

"No," Laura maintained, "because we're friends, not lovers. There won't be any jealousy or heartbreak. Fletcher is free to engage in any relationship he wants. He's been involved in quite a few already, with women I've admired very much, and it hasn't caused the least problem between us."

"What if he became involved with someone you didn't admire? Or someone who resented you and your child's role in his life? Wouldn't you feel that relationship might threaten your child's happiness?"

"I trust Fletcher's judgment. He wouldn't become involved with anyone like that. I also know that he'll put the welfare of our child first and foremost in his life."

"And if he doesn't?"

"He will!"

Cort shifted his gaze away from an indignant Laura. Raising one eyebrow, he asked Fletcher, "What about you? Would you have a problem with Laura becoming... involved...with someone else?"

Fletcher stared at Cort as if he suspected a trap. "I want her to be happy," he replied slowly. "I would never object to any relationship that makes her happy."

Cort nodded, duly impressed. "That's noble of you." He leaned forward, his forearms braced on his knees, his gaze drilling into Fletcher's. "But you haven't exactly answered my question. I didn't ask if you would *object*." Patiently, he rephrased his question. "Would it disturb you to know that she was sleeping with someone else?"

The attention directed at Fletcher suddenly grew intense. Everyone seemed to be scrutinizing him, ready to evaluate the honesty of his answer. Everyone, that was, except Laura, who kept a steady, confident gaze on Cort. She clearly had no doubt about what Fletcher's reply would be, or its validity.

Cort wondered if anyone but him noticed the slight flaring of Fletcher's nostrils or the tightening of his bottom lip. "No," Fletcher finally answered. "It wouldn't disturb me."

The man was lying through his teeth.

Cort allowed a few beats of doubt-heavy silence to pass. Then he smiled—a slow, truce-making smile that had served him well in the boardrooms of the world's wealthiest conglomerates. "Well, then. If that's true, let me be the first to wish you luck with your parenting plan." He extended his hand to Fletcher.

Fletcher blinked, clearly surprised, as if he'd been expecting much more resistance. "Thanks." A flush of relief seeped into his bearded face as he shook Cort's hand.

Cort noticed similar expressions of surprise in the glances the others cast his way, including Laura's. He leaned back in the armchair. "In fact, I'll go one better than just wishing you luck. I'd like to help you get off to the best possible start."

Questions formulated in every pair of eyes.

"What do you mean by 'help'?" asked Fletcher.

"Businesswise. I believe Steffie told me that you're in antiques, Fletcher, and that Laura's in interior design. You're thinking of merging your businesses and buying a commercial building together. Is that right?"

Fletcher nodded. Laura didn't respond, obviously reluctant to discuss her business with him. A refreshing change from the norm, Cort had to admit. Since he'd made his fortune, people had more or less stalked him for the chance to discuss their business ventures.

"I have a sizable chunk of capital that's recently been freed up," Cort said, "and I'm looking to reinvest it." There was no mistaking the flare of interest in Fletcher's gaze. "I wouldn't mind investing in an up-and-coming business like yours. And I wouldn't doubt that you'd be able to use my financial backing."

They stared at him while absorbing the impact of his offer. Financial backing wasn't easy to come by for small retail shops and artistic-service businesses, as Cort well knew.

Laura finally gifted him with a smile—a small, grateful, but regretful smile. "That's very kind of you, Cort, but we really don't need—"

"How sizable an investment?" Fletcher shifted forward on the sofa, a new, aggressive edge to his voice.

Cort shrugged. "Five hundred thousand to start. More, if the circumstances warrant it."

Fletcher drew in a slow, deep breath, then exchanged a wide-eyed glance with Laura, who looked equally shaken at the sum.

Slowly she turned to Cort, her beautiful brown eyes wide with bewilderment. "Why? Why would you offer us this?"

"Because, contrary to what you might believe..." he locked his gaze with hers, allowing her no escape "...I do care about your happiness, Laura."

Her lips parted, her chest rose. Her eyes darkened with some troubled, chaotic emotion.

He wanted very much to kiss her.

"Oh, Cort, you're wonderful!" Steffie cried from where she sat on the arm of B.J.'s chair. "I knew you cared about these guys." She turned a radiant face to the others. "He just gets so wrapped up in business that he forgets to show it."

Laura caught her bottom lip between her teeth and looked away from Steffie.

Cort forced his attention away from Laura's bottom lip and spoke again to Fletcher. "As much as I love to please my sister," he said with a small, self-deprecating smile, "I'm not going to pretend my motives are selfless. I happen to enjoy championing new businesses. Feeding them. Watering them. Watching them grow." He allowed his shoulders to sink deeper into the chair and extended his legs more comfortably in front of him. "Plus, I expect to harvest some healthy financial returns."

Fletcher looked almost faint with excitement, though he tried to maintain a facade of sophistication. "W-would you expect a controlling interest? I mean, Laura and I planned to merge our sole proprietorships into one corporation, but I don't believe we'd be interested in sharing the control with anyone else." He didn't sound very firm on that point. He wouldn't make a very good poker player.

Or a good father for Laura's baby. Every minute that ticked by only strengthened that conviction in Cort.

"Before we finalize my investment," he replied, "I'll need to approve your plans for spending the money. But as far as your business itself goes, I don't want an active role in it. We'll spell out my expectations in the contract. A percentage of the profits. Stock options. Franchise rights. That sort of thing."

Fletcher bestowed another glance on Laura. A speaking glance. An imploring glance. Tiny frown lines gathered between her golden eyebrows and she chewed the bottom corner of her lip, her uncertainty almost painful to behold.

Fletcher swung his attention back to Cort. "We were thinking of buying the building we're in, but there's a renovated mansion nearer to the river that would make the perfect antique shop...and a showcase where Laura could base her design business."

Cort nodded. "I'll have my staff study its commercial potential before you buy it. If you choose the right property, the value should skyrocket in the next few years."

Fletcher turned again to Laura, his excitement palpable. "What do you think, Laur?" He dropped a casual hand on her knee.

Cort tensed at the sight of Fletcher's hand on Laura. The gesture was a casual one, he knew, but also possessive. Husbandly. Who the hell did he think he was?

An obnoxious voice inside his head answered: *The future father of her baby.* A heaviness settled in Cort's gut.

"We'll...we'll talk about it, Fletcher," Laura hedged. "We don't want to jump into anything without a lot of thought."

"Which also makes sense," Cort agreed. "Unfortunately, I can't afford to give you much time. I've got the capital free right now, but I do need to put it back to work. I've had my eye on a few different investment vehicles, and if you decide against my offer, I'll go with one of those. Either way, I'll have to make the move soon."

"How soon?" Sweat beaded on Fletcher's forehead.

"Within the week."

Fletcher blinked behind his wire-rimmed glasses. Laura let out a soft cry. "We have to decide within a week?"

"I'd prefer sooner."

"You two must be out of your minds," Hoss interjected, "not to snap up the offer right now. Money like that don't grow on trees."

"This is the break you've been waiting for, Laura," Tamika urged. "A chance to hire more designers and get your work known. What about that computer system you were talking about?"

"And the advertisements you want to put in magazines?" Steffie added. B.J. and Rory voiced their encouragement, until the noise level rose to a dull roar.

"Stop, stop!" Laura raised her hands in a rather desperate call for silence. It took a moment or two, but the chatter died.

She aimed her gaze at Cort. The resolution in her squared jaw provided an oddly moving contrast with the plea in her eyes. "You're much more experienced when it comes to financial dealings than either Fletcher or I, so I'm asking you as a...a friend, not as a potential business associate."

"A friend?" he repeated softly.

"Yes, a friend," she whispered. She swallowed and he watched the muscles move in her delicate throat. He wanted to press his mouth there, to feel her pulse race beneath his lips. "Does your offer involve *anything* that you haven't made clear?"

He crossed his arms, inclined his head and studied her. "Not that I can think of. You'll want to have your attorneys look over the contract, of course—something I'd insist on, even if you *did* trust me."

Her lips tightened, her chin lifted. "I didn't mean to imply that I don't trust you. I only meant that there might be some aspect of the deal that you haven't fully explained."

"You mean, like...strings attached?"

She didn't reply, and he understood why. She did indeed suspect that he had some "strings" attached to the offer, but Steffie would undoubtedly take offense if she admitted it.

He let her off the hook with an amiable smile and shrug. "I don't know if you'll consider these to be strings, but I will need your cooperation in a few areas that I haven't mentioned. For example, you'll have to incorporate. And you'll have to draw up your business plans in a proposal as part of our contract."

"Sounds reasonable," she allowed. Wariness still blazed in her magnificent eyes. "Anything else?"

"That's it."

She gazed at him in some surprise. Her pent-up breath then eased out and the stiffness left her shoulders. The glance she gave Fletcher contained only a portion of her earlier reserve.

"I do have a favor to ask, though," Cort casually imparted. "Independent of my investment offer, of course."

She slanted him a guarded look. "What kind of favor?"

"I just bought a house in Atlanta. One of those rambling Georgian monstrosities. I believe it's on the historic register." He paused, allowing the image to sink in. "Problem is, I don't have much furniture in it, yet, or carpets, artwork...anything. Other than a couple bedrooms, it's as bare as a barn. I could use some help with the decorating. Since I intend to furnish the place with antiques, I can't think of a better firm to hire than yours."

Dollar signs, he noticed, flashed in Fletcher's eyes.

Cort continued to address Laura. "I'd pay your going rate, whatever it is. I'm planning to entertain my business associates there. Your work would get a lot of exposure to potential clients."

"Georgian architecture?" Laura reflected, her interest undeniably caught. "In Atlanta?"

"Buckhead."

"Buckhead," she breathed. He almost smiled. She obviously approved of the community he'd chosen. "The house wouldn't be designed by Reid, or Shutze, or Crook, would it?" She said the names with a reverence usually reserved for prayer.

"Reid."

A dazzling new luminosity radiated from her face and eyes.

So...she'd responded far more to the artistic challenge than to the lure of big money. He'd have to remember that. He raised an eyebrow. "Are you interested?"

She edged forward on the sofa. "You realize that the process could take quite some time. Weeks, or months, maybe longer, depending what you want to have done. I'll have to send a couple of my designers to study the place, and of course, consult with you. If you won't be available the entire time, you'll have to give them a key and let them—"

"Your designers?" he repeated. He hadn't realized she had other designers working for her.

"Yes. They're very good. Once we have measurements and sketches and photos of the rooms, and you've selected colors, fabrics and styles, we'll work as a team to—"

"Absolutely not." He glared at her, unreasonably put out that she'd even consider sending someone else to decorate his home.

"Pardon me?"

He leaned forward to bridge some of the distance between them, his voice soft, but his gaze unyielding. "I want *you*, Laura. You. No one else."

Her mouth opened, but no words came out.

"If I'm investing in your business, I have a right to see the finished product, and over time, that product will depend on you—not an employee who can leave on a day's notice. I'll give you a key, but I'd like you to stay at the house...with me...for as long as it takes to get the job done."

She still hadn't found her voice.

"I don't think that's asking too much," he said softly, "of a friend." The air between them suddenly felt thick, warm and close. "Besides, Steffie raves about your artistic talent. I'd like to see it for myself. I'm curious to see what you can do. So please..." his gaze played over her face, and his body hardened at the thought of her in his home, alone with him, for days or even weeks "...indulge me. Satisfy my...curiosity."

back to Illinois and don't like the idea anyone will ever guess the truth. Dude, this is a novel. Adrian go work it out, cause she couldn't possibly—"

Adrian laughed out loud, his amusement total.

Cort took a breath.

Laura rushed in. "Dude, Cort, now you two find that you never could blend, but I don't believe there will be to—

CORT KNEW THE BUZZ had started the moment the group dispersed for the night. Carrying his luggage to the bedroom Steffie had assigned him, he imagined he could hear whispers behind every closed door.

He wouldn't escape the buzz for long. They'd find him and discuss their views ad nauseam. Hoping to delay the hashing over of his impulsive propositions until morning, he shut and locked his bedroom door.

He needed quiet time alone. He felt as if a bomb had dropped on him and he needed to piece himself back together. The aftershocks of Laura's plans were still jolting him. Astonishment. Opposition. Self-blame. And a strong, irrational sense of impending loss.

Cursing himself for allowing the feelings at all, he turned to undress for bed, and a quiet knock stopped him. "Cort!" Steffie whispered. "Let me in. I have to talk to you."

He closed his eyes, considered pretending he hadn't heard her, then resigned himself to the inevitable. He opened the door, and his sister sailed in.

"You are so sweet to invest in Laura and Fletcher's business. Any business you touch turns to gold, and they really deserve the boost." She smiled, but anxiety clouded her eyes. "I hope Laura agrees to decorate your house. If she does, can you insist that she start right away? She and Fletcher have an appointment at that clinic next week. We have to find a way to delay them, so we can talk some sense into them. If she has to travel to Atlanta to work at your house, she couldn't possibly—"

Another knock at the door interrupted Steffie.

"Cort, it's me, Tamika." Steffie opened the door, and Tamika rushed in. "Look, Cort, you may say that this is none of my business, but I don't believe Laura will go to your house, and I'm not sure that she should. We'd better come up with a backup plan to slow her down until we can make her see how ridiculous her idea about parenthood really is. They're skipping the love and marriage and going straight for the broken home!"

He stared at the women, perversely amused. They'd both ignored the fact that he'd wished Laura and Fletcher luck with their parenting plan and assumed he disapproved. They were right, of course. He would foil that plan in any way he could. But he hadn't realized that the effort would be part of a widespread conspiracy.

"Why don't you think she'll go, Tam?" Steffie asked.

Tamika plied her with an incredulous stare. "You know as well as I do that she avoids men who show too much interest in her. She's got some internal fire alarm. As soon as she detects serious heat…" she clicked her fingers and pointed at the door "…off she goes. In the opposite direction." Tamika slanted Cort a glance. "Take that as a warning, brother."

He frowned. He'd thought he'd been pretty damn subtle regarding his interest in Laura. "Did it occur to either one of you," he said irritably, "that when I asked her to decorate my house, I had absolutely nothing in mind other than getting my house decorated?"

They glanced at him with barely disguised smirks.

So much for subtlety.

"The way you've been looking at her is enough to send the house up in flames," Tamika retorted.

"I was hoping Laura hadn't noticed," put in Steffie.

"Even if she hasn't and she goes to your house," Tamika went on, "the plan could backfire. Time alone with you could send her rushing to that clinic and her date with a petri dish."

"Thanks." He dropped onto the bed and leaned his back against the headboard. How had he ever come to this? Competing with a damn petri dish!

"Am I correct in assuming that you don't want to see her pregnant by Fletcher any more than we do?" Tamika asked.

The very possibility was making him sick. "I think it would be a mistake," he cautiously admitted.

"It would be a disaster!" Steffie pronounced. "This is her way of slamming the door on romantic relationships. She's made up her mind she doesn't need a lover or a husband, but I believe she does."

"Of course she does," Tamika agreed. "She hides it well, but deep down inside, she's lonely. She needs a man, whether she realizes it or not."

"But once she has that baby, she won't date," Steffie predicted. "She'll use the baby as an excuse. Besides, I'm sure it's harder for a woman with a child to find a man."

"And it won't be beneficial for her child to be the center of her world," Tamika added. "The situation won't do Fletcher any good, either. He never had a mother of his own, and I believe he sees Laura as a mother figure. That can't be healthy."

Cort almost scoffed at that. They might know something about Laura's motivations, but they sure as hell weren't reading Fletcher right. Fletcher wanted Laura tied to him so he could lure her into his bed during a vulnerable moment.

And Cort wasn't about to let that happen. Although her parents' chronic animosity toward each other had probably generated her mistrust of marriage, *he* may have caused, or at least contributed to, her gun-shy view of intimate relationships.

He'd been cruel when he'd left her. Deliberately so. For her own good. She would have sustained much more damage if he hadn't cut their ties. His crime had not been in ending his relationship with her, but in starting it.

He now had to do whatever he could to repair the damage. He had to make her see that physical intimacy didn't necessarily end in emotional pain for either party. If both entered into it with honesty and open minds, an intimate relationship could satisfy profound adult needs. Needs that she really shouldn't ignore....

"So what do we do?" Tamika asked, lifting her palms. As Cort was about to suggest that they butt out and mind their own business, she turned to him. "How about if you make it clear that you won't be home while she's decorating your house? I'm sure she'd go, then. I can stay with her. I'll bring my sweet little Toby and let Laura see how much work a baby can be, and how much emotional support a husband gives, and—"

"Forget it," Cort interjected. "I'm going to be there, at my house. With Laura. Alone." He'd spoken more harshly than he'd intended. Both women looked at him in mild surprise. Tamika tucked her tongue against her cheek.

"I think Laura might accept the decorating job even if he *is* home," said Steffie. "She's very dedicated to her work. And I don't see how a week or so with Cort could backfire. We both agree that she needs to get involved with a man, at least long enough to remind her of what she's missing. Why not Cort?"

Cort wryly shook his head at their assumptions. But he couldn't deny to himself the heat that surged through his blood at the very thought of "reminding her of what she was missing."

"Think, Stef," urged Tamika. "Why has she broken up with every man she's been involved with over the past fifteen years? Why has her longest relationship lasted only a few months?"

"Well, she says she doesn't want to hurt anyone. If she thinks a guy is getting too serious, she breaks off with him for his own good."

"And what made her so sensitive to that kind of hurt?"

"Her parents despise each other. They've made an art form out of keeping each other miserable. And then, of course, she was hurt herself."

"By whom?"

"By—" Steffie stopped and glanced at Cort. Remorse lanced through him. "But that was a long time ago. A silly infatuation, she calls it. She's been over Cort for years! Their past might actually work in our favor. She knows he isn't interested in anything serious, so she won't worry about hurting him. Maybe she'll relax and let things happen."

"I'm so glad you're planning all this out," Cort muttered, trying not to focus on the news that Laura considered their past relationship a "silly infatuation," and that she'd been over him for years. She'd told him as much, of course. *Time proved you right. There was nothing between us except sex.*

The sense of loss bore down on him with renewed force.

"Meanwhile," Steffie continued, unfazed by his sarcasm, "while she's staying with Cort, he can try to talk her out of her parenting plan. And we'll call her and add our two cents' worth, too. We can also work on Fletcher. Make him see how hard it is to raise children. He's the one you should visit with the baby for a week or so."

"Oh, right," Tamika retorted. "Hoss would love that."

"I'd suggest you ladies admit that this entire matter is beyond your control—if you're capable of understanding that concept," said Cort, "and go to bed."

"You *are* going to try to help us talk them out of their parenting plan, aren't you, Cort?" Steffie asked.

Another knock sounded at the door. "Stef? Tamika? Are you in there?"

Cort shut his eyes in weary annoyance.

B.J. stuck her head into the room. "Hoss told me I'd probably find you both here." She strolled in, nudged Cort's outstretched legs aside and plopped down onto the bed. "So, what's the plan? How do we make Fletcher realize that he has to go out and get a life before he fathers a baby?"

An earnest discussion ensued.

Cort, meanwhile, crossed his arms and rested his head against a pillow with his eyes tightly closed. He'd be sure to spend next Thanksgiving in London. Or Rome. Or, hell...Timbuktu.

THE NIGHT PASSED slowly for Laura, yet morning arrived too soon. She wasn't ready to face the day. She'd thought about Cort's offers from every conceivable angle, only to find herself more confused, suspicious and, worst of all, *tempted.*

The chance to make her mark in Atlanta—to design the interior of a Georgian Reid villa—didn't come along every day. Not to mention the half-million-dollar investment in her business, plus profit from decorating the house.

If they made the best of the investment and their businesses flourished, their child would be raised with every advantage that economic freedom could give. How could she walk away from *that?*

Why had Cort offered the money, the job, the exposure? Did he have an ulterior motive, or was she wronging him by suspecting it? She wished she knew!

A discreet knock interrupted her anxious brooding at the early hour of 6:30 a.m. She threw her robe on over her nightshirt and opened the door to admit Fletcher.

He dropped into an armchair while she sat on the edge of the bed. He wore neat blue pajamas, a navy robe, leather slippers and glasses. His well-trimmed beard and tidy morning attire reminded Laura of her father, yet the large, earnest blue eyes behind his glasses brought to mind a little boy. "Do you think Cort is serious about investing that money?"

"I believe so."

"Half a million dollars!" A slight tremor sounded in his voice. "Do you realize what we could do with that kind of cash?"

"Quite a bit." An understatement. They could expand their businesses in the way they'd always dreamed. Take their products nationwide; attract a wealthier clientele.

"So—" he shrugged in bewilderment "—what's the catch? If you didn't think there was one, you wouldn't be hesitating."

She let out a weary breath. "I don't know, Fletcher. Businesswise, I don't believe there is a catch. Cort is a legitimate businessman. He made his fortune by opening and selling small businesses—sports bars, retail shops, coffeehouses. Then he graduated to corporate investments. When you consider all that, his offer doesn't seem unreasonable. And I've never known him to be dishonest. He *is* Steffie's brother. He wouldn't cheat us."

"Then what's the problem?" When she didn't immediately answer, suspicion crept into Fletcher's eyes. "Do you think he'll demand some kind of personal repayment from you?"

"No, he'd never demand that I sleep with him, or anything like that." As she struggled to explain her anxiety, she realized that it stemmed from the fact that Cort would have a role in her life. She would have to deal with him. And she sensed that he wanted her. And he had a way of making *her* want *him*.

Anxiety roiled in her stomach. She couldn't forget the heated determination in his gaze when he insisted he wanted her, and only her, to decorate his home. *Indulge me,* he'd said. *Satisfy my...curiosity.* Curiosity! She'd claimed earlier that she had kissed him out of curiosity. But they'd both known it had been passion—the wild, sexual need that blazed within her the moment his mouth had moved on hers. Had he deliberately referred to their kiss? Had he meant to imply that he expected her to satisfy his passion?

"Maybe *demand* is too harsh a word," Fletcher said, watching her closely. "Would he expect you to sleep with him?"

"Not for the money." How could she explain her vulnerability with Cort? "But he might believe that he was capable of persuading me into it."

Fletcher sprang from the chair and paced, his face ruddy with anger. "I see his game now. He wants to make you feel indebted to him."

"That's not exactly what I meant, but—"

"Let's beat him at his own game, Laur." He turned to her with fierce determination glittering in his baby-blue eyes. "Go decorate his house, and do a fantastic job, and keep it strictly business." With an oddly sardonic twist of his mouth, he said, "*You* shouldn't have any trouble doing that." Laura frowned, vaguely disturbed by the remark, but he went on with angry vehemence, "If he does expect some kind of sexual kickback, it'll serve him right when you turn him down. If he doesn't, we still win...to the tune of half a million dollars."

Laura stared at him in dismay. She couldn't argue with his logic. But logic had little to do with the explosive sexual chemistry between Cort and her.

Silence stretched on between them as an agonized self-debate raged within her. Frown lines etched between Fletcher's eyebrows until he looked pitifully unsure of himself. "You...you don't *want* to go to bed with him, do you?"

"No!" Which was the truth. She did not want to go to bed with Cort Dimitri. She didn't even want to go near him. The doubt on Fletcher's face made her regret mentioning her suspicions. "I've upset you, haven't I? Now you think I'll be in an awkward position if we accept his offer." She reached for his hand and held it. "Don't worry about me, Fletcher. He's not going to force me into anything. And I might be wrong about his motivation. It *is* kind of presumptuous of me to suspect that he'd invest that much money just to...to seduce me."

Fletcher groaned and buried his face in his hands. "I don't know, Laur," he mumbled. "I'd love to have that money backing us. We could own commercial real estate, open more locations, buy merchandise from all over the world." He lifted a tormented gaze to her. "But I don't want you to feel pressured into...anything. You're the one who will be working with him. I've got to leave the decision up to you."

The pained hesitancy in his expression exactly mirrored her own.

FROM THEIR LONG-AGO Hays Street days to their recent reunions, Laura had loved the early-morning hours the group spent lounging over coffee in their pajamas, nightshirts, gowns, robes or—in Rory's case—outlandish boxer shorts. For this morning's selection, he wore little turkeys and pilgrims.

Laura wore her butter-yellow nightshirt and green-plaid flannel robe. She'd hesitated at first to wear her nightclothes to the breakfast table. She'd assumed Cort would be there, and hadn't relished the prospect of socializing with him on such a casually intimate basis. At the last minute, though, she'd changed her mind. Why should she deviate from the tradition she'd enjoyed with her friends over the last fifteen years?

She needn't have worried. Cort was the only one who didn't make his way to the breakfast table that Thanksgiving morning. The rest of them shared fresh bagels, coffee, conversation and laughter.

Curiously enough, no one said much about her plan to have a baby with Fletcher, or Cort's amazing offer. Which probably meant they'd been discussing it among themselves and would be pulling her aside for private chats throughout the day.

Steffie and B.J. soon gravitated toward the raw turkey and argued over how to season it. Tamika went to another room to rock and feed Toby. Hoss read the day's football schedule, and Fletcher and Rory chose the teams they'd bet on.

Laura kept a nervous watch out for Cort while she prepared the stuffing for the turkey. She wanted to talk to him and resolve her doubts about his offer. She had just finished mixing the seasoned cubes of bread with redolent turkey broth, onions and celery when he put in an appearance.

Cort strolled into the kitchen wearing black swim trunks and an unbuttoned, light blue shirt. A towel was draped over one wide shoulder. The very air suddenly seemed charged with raw, potent virility as he walked by. "Morning," he murmured to the group on his way to the coffeepot.

Laura watched him fill a cup with the steaming Frenchroast brew. She willed her heartbeat back to normal before she approached him. "Cort, I'd like a private word with you."

He glanced at her as he set the coffeepot on the burner. His eyes looked strikingly blue this morning; his hair a more lustrous ebony. "Sure. I'm headed to the hot tub in the solarium. We can talk there." His gaze flickered to her nighttime attire, then leisurely rose to meet her eyes in warm invitation. "Why don't you join me?"

She almost dropped the bowl of stuffing.

The hot tub. With Cort. "No, thank you." She was having a hard enough time thinking past the shadowy view of his dark-haired, muscular chest and sleek, hard stomach afforded by his open shirt; the strong, sinewy legs beneath his swim trunks. "I'd like to talk to you before you go in the hot tub, if you don't mind."

He moved a shoulder in a suggestion of a shrug, gripped his coffee cup and sauntered out of the kitchen. Aware of the others watching them, Laura accompanied him down the carpeted corridor, trying to ignore her heated awareness of his commanding size, rugged good looks and masterful aura of confidence that somehow relegated him to leader in any group.

She had no idea how to flush the truth out of him about his motive for making the offer.

She almost jumped at the light touch of his hand at her elbow as he steered her through a doorway. A bedroom, she realized. She'd avoided a hot tub, only to be steered into a bedroom. *Good going!*

It was obviously the room he'd slept in. His clothes from the day before were draped neatly over a chair, his suitcase sat on a cedar chest and the pleasing scent of his aftershave lingered in the air. She looked away from the rumpled bed with sudden sensual awareness. Why should the presence of a bed and Cort in the same room set her pulse to pounding? She'd spent an hour this morning chatting with Fletcher in her bedroom—seated on her unmade bed, yet!—and had never given sensual matters a thought. Unless, of course, she counted her thoughts about Cort and his offer.

Cort shut the door and turned to face her, coffee cup in hand, his manner impersonal; almost aloof. "You wanted to talk?"

She gathered her poise and confronted him. "I don't understand why you offered to invest that money. You can make lucrative deals all over the globe. Why us?"

He sipped his coffee and leaned a shoulder against the door. "I thought I'd explained that last night."

"You said you wanted to do more than just wish us luck with our parenting plan. The usual way to express that sentiment is with a baby gift. A high chair, or crib, or blanket. Not a half-million-dollar investment."

He strolled closer to her, a slight frown in his dark blue eyes. "You're still worried about strings attached, aren't you?"

"No, not strings. I know you have more integrity than

that. But I want to make sure that you're holding no... personal expectations."

"Of course I am."

Her breath caught. "Like what?"

"Healthy profits. A professionally decorated house." He set his cup down on the nightstand and tossed the towel from his shoulder onto a chair. "The pleasure of watching your business grow and knowing I was at least partially responsible."

"I meant, of a personal nature." Her skin tingled with embarrassment. What if she was wrong? How egotistical, accusing him of wanting her enough to invest a half million dollars for the chance to get her alone. It suddenly sounded bizarre, and she hesitated to explain her meaning. But she'd already said too much to back down, and she wanted to hear his answer. "Expectations of a personal nature...between you and me."

His gaze roamed across her face to her unbound hair, then languidly down to her nighttime attire. Traitorous warmth rushed through her at his perusal.

"I suppose I *would* like the chance to get to know you better," he replied. "I mean, I find it damn peculiar that I know you so well in some ways, and not at all in others." His gaze locked with hers and intensified; his voice grew gruff and intimate. "If I close my eyes, Laura, I could pick you out of a hundred women, just by the scent of your skin and hair. And the way you feel against me." He touched her hair, sliding a tendril through his fingers, then smoothed it back with a lingering touch. "But I don't know what kind of music you like, or what makes you laugh, or what you really want out of life." He finished on a whisper, "I'd like the chance to fill in the blanks."

She could barely breathe, so affected was she by the seduction of his words, the heat of his gaze, the stroke of his hand on her hair.

Something like panic flared within her. She'd worked years to fortify herself against such an onslaught; yet one whisper, one touch, had her trembling like the schoolgirl she'd once been.

Anger at him and her own vulnerability fought its way through the sensual haze. "I think you're exactly the same as you always were," she charged, "with one thing on your mind. Except now you're not quite so honest. Now you'll stoop to sweet-talking the women who aren't dazzled by your money."

A spark of anger lit in his gaze. "I haven't met any women who aren't dazzled by my money."

"Oh, yeah? Well, let me introduce myself."

"Please do."

She squared her jaw. "If you were being honest, Cort Dimitri, you would admit that your interest in me hasn't changed. It's still *right here*." She reached down to cup her hand near his crotch, to mimic the insulting gesture he'd made before he'd left her, all those years ago. She stopped just short of touching him.

But his hand shot out reflexively and trapped hers against his body—against the long, hard column beneath his swim trunks.

They stared at each other in stunned silence. Neither had expected this sudden, most intimate of contact. Neither had intended it.

Neither of them moved.

"I never said I didn't want you," he growled, his hardness growing beneath her palm. "I never said that having you here in this room, dressed for bed, with your hair all free and wild, isn't driving me crazy." He frowned and pressed closer. "And if *you* were being honest, Laura Merritt, you would take off that damn robe and whatever you have on underneath it, and make love to me."

Heat pulsated between them.

He released her hand.

She drew away slowly, closed her fingers and held her fist to her chest, her heart thundering. Her palm felt branded by the heat, the size, the hardness that reminded her so vividly of their lovemaking.

He continued to glare at her. "That doesn't mean that's all I want from you, or *for* you. And it doesn't mean we can't work together, in the course of our business, like two reasonable adults."

"I'm not sure that's a good idea." She looked away from him, mortified by her own behavior. She couldn't believe she'd reached for him in such a crude, impulsive way. She hadn't meant to touch him, but when she had, the contact had aroused her. His gaze and words aroused her. Everything about him aroused her. She couldn't trust herself near him!

He cursed beneath his breath and pivoted toward a lace-draped window where milky, snow-filtered light dappled the blue-and-white room. He stood with his back to her. "Laura," he finally said over his shoulder, "you know I would never force you."

"Yes, I know that."

"Can you possibly think I offered half a million dollars to…to *buy* you?"

Embarrassment warmed her face at his incredulous question. She was glad he wasn't watching her. "Of course not."

After another lengthy silence, he turned to meet her gaze. "And is it true that you've been over your 'silly infatuation' with me for years?"

Her heart paused. "Yes."

In tight-lipped silence, he searched her face. "Then why the hell would you even consider turning down my offer?" He studied her as if she were some oddity. "I'm no threat to you, physically or emotionally. You can definitely use the money. And according to what you told me yesterday, you never base important decisions on 'whimsy.' So explain the logic you're using to make this decision."

She wasn't using logic at all. As much as she hated to face that fact, she couldn't escape it. She was afraid of becoming involved with him. Afraid!

Was Tamika right about her? Was she avoiding relationships with men because she was afraid of being hurt again? She'd convinced herself each time that she'd withdrawn for fear of hurting the man. Either way, she couldn't allow her life to be ruled by fear.

But she also couldn't allow herself to be led by lust, which had a way of overpowering her good sense whenever Cort was around.

"You probably wouldn't understand my logic." She knew she sounded patronizing. "My priorities right now are very different from yours. I'm focusing on motherhood."

He crossed his arms, cocked his head and squinted at her, like some superhero employing X-ray vision to examine her soul. "I'd say you have some unresolved issues to face before you take on the challenge of motherhood."

She stared at him in annoyed disbelief. Was he questioning her ability to be a good mother? "What kind of unresolved issues?"

"To start with, your fear of intimate relationships."

"How dare you!" Ignoring that she herself had been pondering that very issue, Laura glowered at him. "You think that just because I'm not falling into bed with you that I'm afraid of intimacy?"

"As a matter of fact, I do."

"If that isn't the most egotistical thing I've ever heard!"

"No, I'd say the most egotistical thing was your insinuation that I was willing to invest *half a million dollars* for no better reason than to take you to bed."

"I never said that."

"But you thought it."

"Ha!" She wished she could force out a real laugh. "If you really want to know, I gave you more credit than that. I believed you were interested in helping my business grow for all the reasons you gave. But I also didn't doubt that you'd take full advantage of the opportunity to lure me to your house and into your bed. Are you going to deny that?"

"Hell, no. We've already established that I want you. I'm not the one in denial. You are."

"Meaning?"

"You want me, too, Laura. I see it in your face when I touch you." His voice turned gruff. "I felt it when you kissed me."

The memory of that kiss glowed and throbbed in her chest. "You've *got* to do something about that ego of yours."

"And you've got to quit kidding yourself—about me, and about Fletcher."

"Fletcher?"

"You said that an affair with another man wouldn't disrupt your relationship with him."

"It wouldn't."

"If you believe that, you're even more naive than you were fifteen years ago."

She drew in a sharp breath, ridiculously hurt that he'd flippantly mentioned the naiveté that he himself had exploited. She clenched her teeth and glared at him. "Is that what you're trying to do? Prove that an affair would disrupt my relationship with Fletcher?"

"No, but I *would* take full advantage of the opportunity if it arose." He didn't even have the grace to look sheepish about it. "Face it, Laura. Sooner or later, you're going to come out of hiding and give some lucky guy all the passion and loving that comes so natural to you."

"I'm not the same girl you used to know."

"Yes, damn it, you are. You might have tried to bury her, but when she breaks free, Fletcher's going to feel that he got a raw deal. He'll resent being saddled with the responsibilities of an ex-husband without ever having enjoyed you as his wife or lover."

"Fletcher wants a child of his own, not me as a wife or lover."

"He wants you the same way I do," he growled, "except he's not man enough to admit it."

His passionate avowal of his desire for her sent rays of heat to her stomach. And a tiny doubt about Fletcher assailed her. *Had* she detected subtle vibes of sensual interest from him? No! He didn't think of her in that way. She couldn't allow Cort to distort her perception of him. Her anger stirred. "I don't want to hear another word about Fletcher."

"Why? Because you might see the truth? He knows you run from intimate relationships, and thinks he's found a back door into your heart that will eventually lead him to your bed. And when you turn to someone else—which you will—your child will be subjected to the same bitterness your parents felt toward each other."

"You barely even know Fletcher!"

"I can see what's on his mind."

"No, you're blinded by what's on *your* mind. And

you've already admitted that you know little or nothing about me."

"You're right. I don't." His voice lost its cutting edge, but none of its heated fervor. "But I do know how you make love, Laura. How you put your whole heart and soul into it...even when it's only a 'silly infatuation.'" His eyes darkened with some new anger before he battled it away. "I will never believe that you've changed that much. If you have, it can't be good for you."

"Oh, you're so noble, worrying about what's good for me. I suppose you're even willing to make love to me to help liberate my suppressed 'inner woman.'"

"I suppose I am."

Once again, she realized she *did* have an unresolved issue to face. Anger! She was deeply, ferociously angry with him, and not only because of the nonsense he was spouting. She'd been living with that anger, trying to deny it, rid herself of it, *protect innocent men from it*, for fifteen long years. This was what she'd been afraid of—waking the beast within her. But the beast had finally opened its eyes and raised its ugly head.

"You hypocrite!" she seethed. "Don't talk to me about fear of intimate relationships. You're the one who used me. Scorned me. Humiliated me!" The truth of her words fanned her wrath. "And then you took off. Abandoned me. Not one phone call, not one letter. Not even a postcard. You forgot I existed!"

"I never forgot you."

She shoved against his chest, furious that even now, she wanted to believe him. "And now you think you can stroll back into my life, murmur pretty words, flash a little cash in my direction and pick up where we left off." The audacity of the man filled her with a rage so sharp and pure, it almost felt like elation. "Then you have the nerve to say you're doing it for my own good!"

She grabbed the nearest weapon—a pillow—and hit him with all her might.

"Laura!" After the first *whummp!* across the face, he dodged and parried with upraised forearms as she wielded the pillow again. *Whummp!* "I've already said I'm sorry." *Whummp!* "You said you forgave me yesterday."

"I lied." *Whummp!*

"Settle down, damn it." He caught hold of the pillow, and she tried to wrest it from him. "You'll have everyone running in here if you don't stop shouting."

"What are you afraid of? That Steffie will realize her saintly brother is a low-down, sorry, bastard son of a bitch?"

He yanked the pillow out of her grasp, threw it aside and captured her arms. "This is good," he reasoned, sounding winded, his hair sticking up at odd angles from her attack. "New territory for us, Laura. We've never fought before."

"I hate you," she raged through clenched teeth.

"I can see we're going to have to work through that."

She struggled in vain to pull away from his iron-strong grip on her arms. "I suppose you'll withdraw your offer," she remarked between angry pants of breath, "now that you know I'd rather die than go to bed with you."

"Die? You'd rather die?"

"Yes, die." She finally shook free of his imprisoning hands and backed out of his reach. Pointing a finger at him, she railed, "If you withdraw your offer now, I'll know you were trying to buy me."

He pressed forward, alarming her, though she refused to show it. "Does that mean you're taking me up on it?"

"I didn't say that."

"If you turn down my offer—" he drew ever nearer "—I'll know you don't trust yourself to be alone with me."

She whirled for the door and flung it open.

A multitude of faces confronted her in the corridor. Steffie stood nearest the bedroom with her fingers fanned across her open mouth. Tamika, a short distance behind Steffie, was frozen in the act of wincing. Rory leaned against the corridor wall, chewing gum and watching with lively interest. Hoss loomed beside him, looking ready to launch into action if necessary. Fletcher hovered in the far distance, his face ashen and anxious.

They'd obviously heard her shouting.

"Today, Laura," Cort called out hoarsely from behind her. "I want your answer today."

Curling her hands into fists, she stalked past her blessedly silent friends and strode to her room.

Cort, meanwhile, closed the door on the several pairs of curious eyes peering in at him. So...Laura hated him, did she? Would rather die than go to bed with him. At least she was finally being honest. Or thought she was.

He, on the other hand, had been less than honest with her.

He'd scoffed at the idea that he would spend half a million dollars to "buy" her. He stared at the far wall, his muscles clenched, his chest tight with reactions too complex to understand. If he thought he could buy her—simply *buy* her—he would. In a heartbeat. Even if it cost him much, much more than half a million.

NEVER IN STEFFIE'S LIFE had a Thanksgiving dinner felt as dismal as this one—except, of course, that terrible year when their mother had been seized and deported to Greece. Cort had been sixteen; Steffie, twelve. They'd dined on cold canned goods in a shabby rented room.

The food this year was superb. The turkey had turned out moist and succulent; the stuffing spicy and delicious; the cranberries, sweet potato casserole, rice, peas and gravy the best she'd eaten in a long time. Even so, she'd almost sighed in relief as dinner drew to a close and she served the pumpkin pie.

It should have been a happy occasion—the fifteenth Thanksgiving dinner shared by the Hays Street gang. But no one seemed to be in much of a celebratory mood. The conversation in her elegant new dining room seemed stilted, the cheerfulness forced.

The tension had started with the quarrel that morning between Cort and Laura. No one really knew what the fight had been about, but they'd heard Laura shouting.

Laura. Shouting!

The rest of them had gaped at each other in disbelief. Laura had called Cort a few choice names that had come through the walls loud and clear. Other than that, they couldn't make out many words. Afterward, Laura had resisted confiding in anyone. So had Cort. And Fletcher.

Poor Fletcher! He looked pale, nervous and miserable, sitting there beside Laura and sneaking surreptitious glances across the table at Cort. Steffie couldn't tell if Fletcher was suspicious about the offer Cort had made, or concerned that Laura's quarreling had endangered that offer, or hurt by the realization that no one but Rory approved of him fathering Laura's baby.

Friction among the Hays Street gang was a new phenomenon. Steffie didn't like it.

She was tempted to pull Cort away from the table and ask him to call off the scheme they'd discussed last night to make Laura and Fletcher break their appointment at the clinic. As much as she wanted time to talk them out of their parenting plan, she suddenly felt uneasy about Cort's involvement. What if Tamika was right, and the time Laura spent with him made matters worse?

She supposed she shouldn't worry. After that quarrel, Laura probably wouldn't go to Cort's house, and he probably wouldn't go through with the investment deal.

Steffie almost sighed again as she dug her fork into her slice of pumpkin pie. She'd hoped Cort and Laura would become friends again. Or more than friends. It seemed unlikely now that they'd ever even speak to each other again. Laura had clearly been avoiding him since this morning, spending all her time with Tamika's baby, or decorating the table with little pumpkins, stalks of wheat and horns o' plenty that she'd brought with her in her suitcase. Cort hadn't made a single move to engage her attention.

A silence had fallen over the dining room while everyone concentrated on pie and coffee. Steffie almost dropped her fork when Laura suddenly broke that silence.

"Cort," she said in her low, soft voice that Steffie had never heard raised in anger until that morning. "Fletcher and I have made up our minds regarding your investment offer."

Fletcher turned his head so fast he choked on a mouthful of pie and coughed into his napkin, still gaping at Laura.

Cort stirred a teaspoon of sugar into his coffee, took a long, leisurely swallow, then set the cup back down. He didn't act nearly as interested in their decision as everyone else seemed to be. "Yeah?"

Laura angled her chin. Steffie knew that meant she was nervous, but somehow the tilt to her chin always made her seem serenely composed. "If you'll draw up the contract, we'll have our attorney look it over."

Cort reached for the serving bowl of whipped cream and spooned a dollop of it onto his pie. He didn't even glance in Laura's direction. "Does that mean you intend to decorate my house?"

She raised her chin a little higher. "Yes."

He picked up his fork, dipped it into the sweet pumpkin filling and brought a creamy mound to his mouth. That's when he looked at her...while he filled his mouth with the pie and slowly drew the fork out empty. He locked gazes with her, as if they were the only two people in the room...the way he had back in the Hays Street house.

Steffie hadn't seen him look at anyone else with quite the same intensity.

He took his own sweet time chewing that pie, rolling it around in his mouth, savoring it in a lazy, lingering way before he swallowed. "Monday," he said. "I want you there Monday."

Laura indulged in a long, slow sip of her coffee, even though she hadn't put cream or sugar in it, as she always did. Warm color had climbed into her cheeks, and when she spoke, her voice sounded throaty and breathless. "I can't possibly make it before Friday."

"I'm on a tight schedule. Tuesday's the latest we can start."

"I'm sorry, but I have an appointment to keep midweek."

His fingers tightened around the handle of the china coffee cup, and Steffie winced, remembering what had happened to the stem of her brandy snifter last night. Cort's gaze darkened, but his voice came out softer, gentler, than it had been. "You'll have to postpone your appointment."

A stubborn, willful light leaped in Laura's eyes.

Steffie found herself holding her breath. The appointment, as everyone at the table knew, had to do with her conceiving Fletcher's baby.

Fletcher seemed to be holding his breath, too. As Laura's

gaze took on a stormy look and the adversarial tension mounted, Fletcher piped up, "Uh, Cort. That starting date. Is it set in stone? You know…a deal breaker?"

"'Fraid so."

Sweat gathered on Fletcher's forehead. "Um, Laura…" He turned to her and cleared his throat. She shifted her gaze away from Cort and trained it on Fletcher. "We can postpone the appointment," he murmured in a near whisper. "A month, just a month. I mean, what would it hurt?"

They exchanged a long, private, meaningful gaze. Fletcher looked as if he was silently pleading.

With a slight tightening of her lower lip, Laura swung her attention back to Cort. Her chin again tilted in that regal way of hers. "Okay," she whispered. "Tuesday."

Cort didn't smile, or reach to shake their hands, or say anything at all. He just stared at Laura.

She set her napkin beside her plate and left the table.

Steffie released the breath she'd been holding and rose to clear the dishes away. Tamika and B.J. helped. Hoss and Rory ushered Fletcher into the other room to watch football, and Cort walked off toward the bedrooms.

Steffie set the dishes aside and followed him. She had to talk to him about her concern that maybe Tamika was right. Maybe he shouldn't stay at home while Laura decorated his house. If the tension she had felt between them was anything to judge by, someone could end up hurt.

He hadn't closed his bedroom door all the way, and Steffie poked her head in. He stood near the window with his back to her, talking on his cell phone. "That's right," he was saying. "Move everything out of the house. The furniture, the carpets, the artwork. Everything. Put it all in storage. I want the house bare."

Steffie listened in surprise.

"Oh, but leave my bed. Yes, just the bed." After a slight pause, he added in a somewhat grudging tone, "And a bed in the guest room. The one directly across the hall from mine."

5

CORT REALIZED WITH an oddly remote portion of his brain
that some form of insanity must have come over him.

He'd left Steffie's house Friday, flown home and rear-
ranged his schedule—postponing important meetings,
delegating crucial tasks, freeing up his time. He then su-
pervised the move of his home furnishings, which took a
ten-man crew the entire weekend. He'd left a few func-
tional pieces in the kitchen, his bedroom and the guest
bedroom, along with his favorite Oriental carpets and antique pieces scattered throughout various rooms—more
than he'd originally planned to leave. Otherwise, he'd
stripped the mansion bare.

And all the while, he thought about her. He wondered if
she'd really come, or if she'd change her mind. He wondered how she felt about their deal; about staying with
him; about their heated words on Thanksgiving morning.
He wondered if her anger would stop her from ever opening herself to him again.

As he tossed restlessly in bed on Monday night, a new
concern hit him. What if his interference with her clinic appointment had backfired? What if she'd decided to forgo
the artificial insemination and sleep with Fletcher?

Sharp, hot talons of anxiety clutched him. He spent the
night pacing, sweating and visualizing torturous scenar-
ios.

She and Fletcher had returned to Memphis on Friday afternoon, according to Steffie. They'd said they had a lot to arrange before Laura left for Atlanta. They needed to utilize all of the short time they had. Did that include their nights?

Why the hell did it matter so much to him, anyway? His world wouldn't end if she was, at this very moment, sharing another man's bed. Holding him in her arms. Taking him into her body. Cort's breath wedged like a stone at the base of his throat. His life wouldn't change if she conceived another man's child...and spent her life tied to that man in a profoundly elemental way....

The night dragged by, second by excruciating second.

LAURA AWOKE with a start, her sleep disrupted by the snoring of the man next to her. She lifted her head from the pillow, startled to find herself somewhere other than her own bed.

The plane, she realized. She'd fallen asleep on the plane. Relaxing again in the narrow seat, she turned away from the stout, dozing passenger beside her and gazed through the window at the cottony clouds below. The short nap had been the most restful sleep she'd had all weekend. She'd spent her time preparing her business for her absence, amassing the materials she would need for the job and rationalizing her decision to accept Cort's offer.

No matter how profound her reservations, no matter how much he had hurt her in the past, she simply hadn't been able to walk away from the financial advantages his investment would mean for Fletcher and her. The benefits would, in turn, translate into added security for their future child. She also hadn't been able to dismiss the exposure her work would get if she decorated Cort's house in Atlanta. The practical side of her demanded she take advantage of this once-in-a-lifetime opportunity.

The not-so-practical side of her had kept her awake every night agonizing over Cort. *You're afraid to be alone with me,* he'd said. God help her, it was true. He had the power to affect her in ways no one else could.

In the fifteen years they'd been apart, no one else had hurt her as deeply. No one else had succeeded in inciting her passion to a feverish pitch. No one had riled her into a rage. She'd shouted at him! Told him she hated him. Hit him, for heaven's sake. The fact that she'd attacked him with a pillow made the assault no less shocking.

She'd behaved in the same despicable way her parents treated each other. She'd never understood or approved of their relationship, but now she'd gleaned an uncomfortable insight. For even when she'd been yelling at Cort, her anger hot and fierce, she'd felt more vibrantly alive than during her finest moments with any other man.

A frightening realization. And that was why Cort scared her—he'd turned her into someone else. Someone with wild, volatile passions that secretly thrilled her. Someone she didn't know how to control.

You've tried to bury her, Cort had charged, speaking of the passionate girl she had once been. She supposed that was true. She had worked hard to make herself wiser and less vulnerable. Had she also buried a part of herself that clamored to be free?

You have unresolved issues to face before you take on the challenge of motherhood. Did she? Were those "unresolved issues" the reason Cort wielded so much power over her? The reason she hadn't given her heart to any other man? She'd been telling herself that she didn't need a lover or a husband, but...did she?

The questions shook her. They were too important to leave unanswered. So important, she suddenly realized, that she couldn't go through with her parenting plan until she'd answered them. She had to be settled and secure within herself before she brought a baby into the world. No child of hers would be subjected to the turmoil caused by an emotionally needy parent.

Until Cort had come back into her life, she'd felt strong, stable and secure. And alone. Wasn't that why she wanted a baby so badly—to fill the empty place in her heart, in her arms, in her life? She couldn't deny that she'd been lonely.

Had she also been sexually repressed?

Laura stared out of the airplane window and ground the knuckles of her fist against her chin. The way she'd been obsessing over Cort certainly led her to believe so. Sexual repression—or simple obsession, for that matter—were warning signs she couldn't ignore. She needed to understand this volatile part of herself before she conceived a baby. She had to diffuse the tension that gripped her whenever Cort was near, and to learn the meaning of the power he held over her. To proceed with her parenting plan without understanding these things would be unfair to Fletcher, her future baby and herself.

If necessary, she would postpone her appointment at the clinic yet again. She was hoping, though, that she could find answers to her questions and put to rest her doubts during this trip to Atlanta.

You realize what you're contemplating, don't you? she asked herself. *Sex. With Cort!* He would be the logical partner to help her explore her repressed sexuality. Her "inner woman" took on a life of its own whenever he was around. She obviously had to draw that passionate inner woman to the surface where she could face her. Understand her. Find a comfortable way to live with her.

She had no doubt at all that her inner woman would lead her to Cort's bed. The idea both terrified and titillated her.

It also presented a problem, she suddenly realized. Perhaps an insurmountable problem. In preparing for motherhood, she'd cleansed her body of all contraceptives. As her chart clearly indicated, she was approaching her most fertile time of the month.

She couldn't risk getting pregnant by the wrong man! Nothing would be worse than that!

By the time the plane landed, Laura was feeling torn, apprehensive, ruthlessly repressed and dangerously obsessed with thoughts of making love to Cort.

Not a good mind-set for the first day on the job.

AFTER A HELLACIOUS NIGHT of imagining the worst about Fletcher and Laura's nocturnal activities, Cort rose early on Tuesday feeling tense, impatient and unwilling to wait for Laura to arrive at his house, as they'd planned.

He needed to see her again, and soon. No sense wasting the hour it would take for her to rent a car and drive across town. A call to the airlines provided him with her flight number, and he sped all the way to the airport.

Would she be there, or had she changed her mind?

He parked near the curb, paid a security guard a healthy sum to keep an eye on his open-topped car and strode into the terminal, his eyes peeled as he searched the crowd. With a crazy kick of his heart, he spotted her in baggage claim. Relief slowed him to a standstill. He needed a moment to relax the uncomfortable tautness in his muscles and jaw. To regain the nonchalance he'd somehow lost. To drink in the sight of her.

She stood waiting for her luggage to appear on the moving carousel, her coat draped over her arm. She wore a taupe sweater dress that clung to a few choice curves, yet draped with subdued elegance over others. The hemline reached below her knees. Her high heels accentuated the shapeliness of her long, slender calves, making him hunger to see more of her legs. It had been too damn long since he'd seen them...or felt them wrapped around him.

A familiar longing tightened his loins. She always seemed to have that effect on him.

She turned her head to smile at a child standing beside her, and Cort noticed that her honey-blond hair glistened in a soft, loose twist—the kind that might tumble down in a silken rush at the removal of a single hairpin. Small gold studs glinted at her ears, drawing his gaze to the clean, elegant lines of her jaw and throat. He'd kissed her there at least a thousand times.

She laughed at something the child said, her face radiant with gentle amusement. Cort had never seen her looking more beautiful. He'd never felt such a strong possessiveness; a need to let the world know that she belonged to him.

Belonged to him. Except she didn't.

She leaned to reach for a large leather suitcase moving toward her on the conveyor belt. He crossed the short distance, stepped in behind her, hooked his hand into the handle of the suitcase and swung it from the carousel.

"Oh," she cried, her wide brown eyes watching the suitcase. "Excuse me, sir, but that's—" Her protest died when her gaze reached his face. "Cort," she breathed.

She looked flustered at the sight of him. Or maybe just surprised. The subtle rise of color in her cheeks, the parting of her lips, the lingering sweep of her gaze across his face—none of it necessarily meant that she felt the same pull of emotion that he did at seeing her again.

The last time they'd been alone, she'd said she hated him.

"I...I didn't expect you to be here." She managed a small smile and nervously raked a wayward tendril of her hair back with her fingers. "I thought we'd agreed that I'd rent a car."

"I didn't see any sense in that when I have a few you can choose from."

She hesitated, as if searching for a reason to argue. An excuse not to go with him.

It took every ounce of his willpower not to pull her into his arms and kiss some sense into her—or out of her. He hadn't lost his mind entirely, though. He was fully aware that one wrong move could send her running back to Fletcher.

Anxiety cut through his chest. Had they set their parenting plan into action? Could she, even now, be carrying Fletcher's baby? Cort shoved the bothersome questions to the back of his mind. She was with *him* now, in *his* world, and at the moment, nothing else mattered but keeping her here. "Is this all of your luggage?"

"The rest is there." She gestured toward another large suitcase, a boxed crate and an overnight bag. "I've brought a few catalogs to show you. And software. Fabric, paint and carpet samples."

"Good." He *had* to touch her, or some internal organ of his would burst with the pressure of resisting. So he gestured to a skycap to handle the crate and luggage, settled a hand at her waist, near the small of her back, and steered her through the crowd.

He reluctantly let go of her as she presented her baggage-claim tickets to a guard at the door, who checked the numbers and waved them through. Silently they trekked along a busy sidewalk, into the fresh, balmy Georgia breeze.

She lifted her face to the bright morning sun. "The weather's so beautiful. Feels more like May than late November."

"Let's hope it lasts. In Atlanta, you never know. Next week might be in the eighties, or we could have snow."

"That's true. We never knew what kind of weather to expect for Thanksgiving or Christmas."

He'd almost forgotten that she'd grown up in an Atlanta suburb. Casually he caught hold of her arm and guided her toward his car. "Why did you leave Georgia?" he asked her, curious.

"Grad school. I guess the thing that appealed the most to me about attending an out-of-state university was all the mileage between my parents and me."

He didn't doubt that. He remembered how upset she'd always been by her parents' occasional visits—usually prompted by their decision to divorce, which never bore fruit. At least, not while he'd known her. "Do your parents still live here?"

"No. In Florida. My mother hates the heat and mosquitoes, so my father bought a condo near the Everglades." A sardonic sparkle lit her eyes. "She gets back at him by spending too much money and flirting with the neighbors."

Nothing much had changed on the home front. "How did Fletcher wind up in Memphis?"

"He stopped by to visit me during one spring break and liked the place so much, he decided to live there."

Liked the place so much. Cort gritted his teeth. She could have been on a frozen tundra and the guy would have decided to live there. "Did he have a problem with you coming here—" his voice grew unavoidably huskier "—staying with me?"

Laura turned a searching glance on him. Why, she wondered, was he asking? Had he noticed something in Fletcher's demeanor before they'd left Steffie's, or was he simply trying to further his contention that Fletcher felt more for her than friendship?

"Of course he didn't mind," she replied. "He's thrilled." Not exactly a lie. He *had* been thrilled at the prospect of all that money, but also anxious regarding her stay with Cort. His concern, Laura knew, had been prompted by her hesitation to accept Cort's offer. Fletcher hadn't wanted her to feel pressured or put into an awkward position.

Little did he know how awkward that position really was. Her newly realized need to explore her repressed sexuality warred with the defenses she'd built up over the years. The conflict grew more desperate with every glance at Cort, every elusive whiff of his appealing, masculine scent, every casual touch of his hand. The warm southern sunshine and the smell of Georgia pines didn't help, either, evoking memories of the love-crazed days they'd spent together.

She couldn't help seeing him as the intense young man he'd been—the street-toughened loner whose every hard-earned penny went to pay for the house, food and tuition for his kid sister. Looking back, Laura realized he'd carried quite a weight on his young shoulders. She hadn't fully appreciated that at the time.

Emotion stirred in her heart. A sudden desire to touch him, hold him. A tingling of fear...

He stopped beside a car, nodded to a nearby security guard and unlocked the trunk for the skycap to load her luggage.

Soon they would be alone.

"A convertible," Laura remarked, glad for the distraction presented by the handsome, gleaming, butter-yellow automobile.

Cort escorted Laura to the passenger door and slanted her a curious glance. Did she know it was a Rolls-Royce

Corniche convertible, and a very limited model at that? If
so, she gave no sign as she settled into the soft, fragrant
leather seat. If she knew, would she enjoy the ride more?
Disapprove of the extravagance? Think he was trying to
impress her?

Cort realized with a start that he *was* trying to impress
her. To "dazzle her," as she'd put it. Ensconce her in luxury beyond any she'd ever experienced.

What the hell was wrong with him? He'd moved beyond that stage of his life, when the approval of others had
meant something to him. He no longer strove to impress,
please or gratify...except to gain a psychological advantage in business. On a personal level, he didn't give a
damn who liked what.

"Do you know how long it's been since I rode in a convertible?" A smile of anticipation curved her lips. "Thank
goodness it's warm enough to ride with the top down."

An irrepressible gladness rose in him. He *had* pleased
her. With a wry, self-deprecating shake of his head, he
took his place behind the wheel, guided the Rolls out of the
airport, turned away from the expressway and headed
down a back road, toward a scenic route.

The wind roared above their heads; the loose tendrils of
her hair whipped wildly about her face and she dazzled
him with a smile of pure enjoyment.

"Does this mean you don't hate me anymore?"

"Not at the moment," she temporized.

He smiled, and they rode in companionable silence for
quite a few miles. They stopped at a red light, and he noticed a paperback book wedged in a side pocket of her
purse: *Preparing For Pregnancy*.

Dismay pulsed through him, and the topic he'd been
struggling to forget roared to the forefront of his mind. He
tried to think of a way to broach the subject. Not an easy

thing to do. He couldn't very well ask, *Did you, by any chance, sleep with Fletcher?*

Instead, as they waited at the intersection for the light to change, he remarked, "Sorry I couldn't be more flexible with our starting date. I know you had to cancel your appointment. Were you, uh, able to reschedule?"

After a slight hesitation, she replied, "Don't worry about the appointment. I'm not."

He turned in his seat to face her. What the hell was that supposed to mean? Why wasn't she worried about it? Because she'd slept with Fletcher and no longer needed the clinic's services?

Another possibility occurred to him then; one he preferred to believe. One that he could actually ask her about. "Does that mean you've decided against your parenting plan?"

Her cheeks took on a rosy hue. "No, I haven't decided against it. I only meant that my appointment is not a top concern of mine at the moment. So please, forget it."

A tight, heavy ball formed in his chest. He couldn't possibly forget it. "Laura..." He struggled to find a delicate way of phrasing the question he had to ask. "Is there a chance that you're...already pregnant?"

"Already pregnant?" She whipped a startled gaze to him. "Of course not. I haven't been to the clinic at all yet." Her eyes widened. "Oh! You mean..." Her color heightened. "No! Fletcher and I have agreed that we wouldn't...I mean, we feel very strongly that we shouldn't...well..."

"Good." Never had a piece of information filled him with such intense relief. He felt almost light-headed with it. "That's smart. Mixing sex and parenthood...well, it's...it's just not a good idea."

"Oh, I know." She nodded in agreement.

He firmly shut his mouth and tried not to wince. *Had he*

ever said anything more stupid? The car behind him honked and he realized that the traffic light had changed to green. Turning his gaze back to the road, he said, "What I meant was, sex could really mess up a relationship that's based on parenthood, just like parenthood could mess up a relationship that's based on sex." There. At least that made sense.

"Yes, but can we please change the subject now?" She glared at him in mild exasperation. "I feel uncomfortable talking about this with you."

Uncomfortable. She felt uncomfortable talking about her pregnancy plans with him, but perfectly at ease *making* those plans with Fletcher. Perfectly at ease *making a baby* with Fletcher.

Cort couldn't stand the thought.

They lapsed into silence as he turned off the side road and drove down a busy stretch of Peachtree Street, past restaurants, nightclubs and congested shopping areas. It wasn't until they were riding down wide, tree-canopied residential roads that either of them spoke again.

"Cort?" she called over the noise of the wind, peering through the windshield toward the hood ornament. "Is this..." she hesitated, her golden eyebrows drawn together "...a Rolls-Royce?"

Glad for the distraction from his thoughts and pleased that she'd finally noticed the car, he nodded. And waited for a comment. None came.

When he glanced at her again, she was gazing at the lush green scenery and the sprawling old mansions, her expression giving no clue as to her reaction. Vaguely disappointed, he reminded himself that she never had been one to pay much attention to cars. Back in their Hays Street days, he'd considered that a blessing. He'd been lucky to own a twelve-year-old clunker with a threadbare interior and a jammed passenger door.

An unpleasant memory surfaced of the cars her other admirers had driven. Porsches, Corvettes, classic sports cars. Rich boys who had known her from her college classes, with their wallets full of cash to take her places he could never afford to take her.

She hadn't gone with them. She'd spent her free time with him, between his two jobs and her classes. The places they'd gone together hadn't required a car, or money. Or clothes.

He found himself gripping the steering wheel with unnecessary force as he turned into the elegant, woodsy neighborhood where he lived. He wanted to lavish her with luxuries now. Spoil her so badly that only a very, very rich man could afford her.

But she hadn't been visibly impressed with his car.

What would she think of his house?

As they motored up the driveway that wound between towering hardwoods and massive magnolias, he tried to see his home through her eyes. Through the widely spaced trees, across a rolling grassy knoll, the white stucco mansion came into view, surrounded by smoothly mounded boxwoods, blooming camellias and lush winter gardens.

He'd bought the place because of the investment value and the serenity of the neighborhood, but mostly because he'd fallen in love with it. The house, the woods, the gardens stirred a vague, restless yearning in him that somehow brought to mind warm, golden feelings from long ago. A need had seized him to share this sense of place, of home, with someone close to his heart.

But he had no one close to his heart...except Steffie, who'd been busy with her job and mired in divorce proceedings at the time he'd bought the place.

Although he was careful not to look directly at Laura as he parked the car in the circular driveway, he surreptitiously watched her. She gazed at the house with patent interest, but remained stoic and silent.

He had no idea how she, a connoisseur of architecture and design, would perceive the place. He himself knew little about aesthetics. He recognized a solid investment when he saw one, but what did he know of truly fine things?

Growing up, he'd been exposed to grandeur only through the back stairwells of the houses in which his mother had worked as a housekeeper. That glimpse of elegance had given way to the grimness of shabby apartments and inner-city streets.

He'd had no cultured upbringing, and money couldn't buy one. The wealthy impressed each other not with the making of the money, but with the spending of it. He was a newcomer at the art.

Maybe he'd made a mistake in describing the house to her. Maybe he'd raised her expectations in a way he didn't understand.

He led her up the flight of stairs, unlocked the door and gestured for her to precede him. She stepped into the tiled, circular entrance hall and gazed around at the high ceilings, the curved staircase and the ornate archways that led to the main rooms. He hung back, allowing her to take the lead. He could have directed her through the house, pointed out the features that had impressed him, but he didn't.

He shoved his hands into his pockets and followed her. Although he'd been present for the moving of his furniture, he still hadn't gotten used to the vast emptiness of the place. The echoes of their footsteps added to the disconcerting sense of the unfamiliar.

She took her time looking around. When they had toured through most of the main level, she stopped in the one downstairs room that contained a carpet and piece of furniture—the library, a massive chamber with dark, carved woodwork gracing walls of built-in bookcases. An antique mantel presided over a tiled fireplace. A cream, rose and gold Oriental carpet spread nearly wall-to-wall over the hardwood flooring.

Her gaze traversed the rich landscape of the room, then locked with his. Still, she said nothing. He struggled to keep his patience. Common courtesy required a comment of some kind, damn it. He was very near demanding one.

Then he noticed a sheen springing to her eyes. She pivoted away, as if to study the antique mantel.

"Laura?" He frowned, pressed closer and peered around her shoulder to see her face. "Are you disappointed with the house?"

"Of course not. It's..." she swallowed spasmodically "...beautiful," she croaked.

He stared at her in absolute confoundedness.

She averted her face again, and after a moment, in a strained voice that seemed to be holding back tears, said, "How could I be disappointed? The details are exquisite. Like the carving in here—the mantel, the cornices, the overdoor swags. It's the work of a master carver. Probably Millard."

He nodded. He'd been told as much.

She faced him, her eyes glossy, her bottom lip noticeably taut. "And did you know that the tile in the dining room mantel is James M. Beath's artwork?"

"No, I didn't know," he replied cautiously. "But that's not a bad thing, is it?"

"And the chimney breast in the drawing room...well, it's..." she shrugged, as if unable to find words "...it's a nineteenth-century masterpiece." A tear escaped and rolled down her cheek.

Bewildered, frustrated and helpless in the face of feminine tears, he spread his hands out wide. "Then what's wrong?"

"Nothing," she whispered, dashing away a teardrop as another formed. "It's just that I remember when you slept on a mattress on the floor because you didn't have a frame and box spring. And you drove a c-crummy old Chevy with a cracked windshield, and sometimes ate peanut butter sandwiches or oatmeal for days."

"But what does that have to do with—"

"You said you *liked* peanut butter sandwiches and oatmeal. I used to think that was s-so cute. I never really understood that you just couldn't afford—"

"I was a kid back then," he interjected, annoyed by the memories he preferred to forget. "None of that meant anything."

"It *did* mean something. You worked six days a week running that bar and grill, and the night shift at a factory."

"So what? I needed the money."

"Yes, you did." She smiled at him through her tears with such affection his heart stood still. "Yet you bought Steffie everything she needed. You insisted she stay in school. And when any of the others were having problems and couldn't come through with their share of the rent, you never hassled them. You let them live in the house until they could pay. The electric company turned off the lights one time and your car was almost repossessed, but you..."

"I did what I had to do," he cut in, uncomfortable with the direction of the conversation. "Nothing more, nothing less." If she knew the things he'd resorted to during the worst of times—before she'd even met him, actually—she wouldn't think much of him at all.

"You're getting upset just thinking about being broke, aren't you?" Her voice sounded tight and tear-laden again. "I knew you would. Like that Christmas when I gave you a leather jacket and you wouldn't take it. You said you forgot to buy me anything." Fresh tears welled up. "But I saw the box you shoved under the mattress." Her lips trembled. "It was a scarf."

He gaped at her, incredulous that she'd known about that cheap, silly gift he'd hidden from her. "You opened it?"

"It was a *beautiful* scarf," she whispered harshly.

He closed his eyes, almost as humiliated now as he would have been back then. "I bought it at a drugstore for a couple of bucks."

"I would have loved it."

He clenched his jaw against a swell of self-directed anger. He shouldn't have bought the damn thing to start with. It might have fallen apart around her neck, or the dye might have stained the expensive clothes she always wore. At least, they'd seemed expensive to him back then. "For God's sake, Laura, that was fifteen years ago. You're upset with me *now* for not giving you that scarf?"

"You think I'm upset because I wanted the scarf?" She stared at him as if he'd lost his mind. "The scarf has nothing to do with it!"

Never, never would he understand this woman! He gripped her by the shoulders and sat her down beside him on the immense Italian-leather sofa, one of the few pieces of furniture he'd chosen to keep. "Then why in the hell," he demanded in soft, wretched puzzlement, "are you crying?"

She seemed to get choked up all over again. "Because

you thought I would think less of you for giving me an inexpensive gift. You thought it would be better to say you forgot to buy me one at all." Her brown eyes shimmered. "And now you have so much. Millions of dollars, the finest of cars, the most b-beautiful house I've ever seen."

Despite his concern and bewilderment, gladness seeped into his chest. *The most beautiful house she'd ever seen.* So she *was* affected by the place, the same way he was. Which meant he wasn't entirely delusional in believing he could keep her happy here.

He tightened his grip on her shoulders and pulled her closer, moving his hands in a lightly kneading massage, savoring the warm, vital feel of her. "My rise in fortune is a good thing, Laura," he whispered, caressing her forehead with his chin. "Trust me on this."

She pulled back and gazed at him with an agonized tenderness that spread warmth to every part of his body. "Yes, and I'm happy for you. But the way you were watching me, waiting to see if I liked your car and your house..." another tear spilled over her spiky lower lashes "...as if my approval meant something so...so personal...."

Her insight disturbed him. Her approval did mean something very, very personal to him. How could he explain that, though, when he barely understood it himself?

"I get the feeling," she whispered, "that you believe these fine, expensive things are more important than they really are."

"No, hell no," he gruffly reassured her, glad for something he could honestly deny. "Things are just things." He slid his hands along her damp, silken face, cradled it between his palms and gently wiped away her tears with his thumbs. He still hadn't grasped the exact cause of her anguish, but she felt strongly enough about it to cry—and it was clearly over him. The warmth within him turned needful.

"You can afford to give a woman incredible gifts now," she went on with a catch in her tremulous voice, "that might even change her life. But that could mean that you never recognize the most valuable thing you have to offer."

Distracted by a need so great it made him dizzy, he angled his head and pressed his lips to her tear-dampened cheek. He'd waited so long to feel her skin beneath his mouth again. The sweet, salty, velvet texture filled him with a delicious ache.

"I'm afraid you'll sell yourself short," she whispered.

He murmured a vague, fervent promise and brushed his mouth down the curve of her face, lost to everything but the feel, the scent, the taste of her.

She closed her eyes. Parted her lips. And drew in a long, audible breath.

By the time he reached her mouth, he was hot, hard and driven. Deeply, passionately, he kissed her.

6

LAURA SLID HER ARMS around his neck and sank into the sultry pleasure of his kiss. She needed this—the hot, intimate contact with him; the deep, urgent thrusting of his tongue; the flare of answering fire within her. Ah, yes, she needed this!

The pressure in her heart had grown too great to bear otherwise. He had watched her through dark, veiled eyes, waiting for her reaction to his car and house as if her approval meant something personal and vital. The vulnerability seemed so at odds with his toughness, his strength, his unwavering self-assurance.

She ached with the knowledge of that secret vulnerability, because she wasn't the person who could fill his underlying need. He'd told her so before he'd left her—*I don't love you, Laura.* And isn't that what she believed he needed—someone to love, someone who would love *him*? Isn't that why she had cried—because she feared his riches would buy him someone who didn't?

The sensuous play of his tongue in her mouth coaxed her away from her emotional turmoil, distracting her with seductive sensations she felt only with him; the hot, virile flavor she tasted only in his kiss. He could lure her so easily into the sweetest delirium.

But she pulled back, too troubled to let herself go. "I told you last week that I hated you." Anxiously she searched his swarthy, rugged face. "You...you don't think I'm kissing you now because of your car or your house, do you?"

A glimmer of amusement flashed through the fierce desire in his gaze. "You're forgetting my ego." He pulled the pins from her hair and freed it to tumble in an unruly cascade around her shoulders. Weaving his fingers through its heaviness, he returned his stare to hers. The amusement had fled, leaving only serious heat. "I'm egotistical enough to believe that you'd be kissing me," he whispered hoarsely, "even if I were some poor factory worker with a beat-up old Chevy and peanut butter for every meal."

An emotion too strong to be called tenderness overpowered her, and she met him in a hard, openmouthed kiss. His arms came around her, crushing her to him. She reveled in the muscled breadth of his chest; the strength of his body; the arousingly masculine scent of his skin.

He groaned and pushed her down onto the sofa.

Their kisses grew longer, more voluptuous. She'd forgotten how intoxicating the taste of him could be. How each kiss heightened the need to merge with him; to draw him in ever deeper. How the longing could grow desperate.

The parry and thrust turned too rough, too needful. He drew back with a hard exhalation of breath, his stare smoldering through the sensual haze he'd submerged her in. "I never forgot you, Laura," he rasped. "I never stopped wanting you."

She believed him, because she'd never stopped wanting him. Heat and emotion seared through to her heart, and she tangled her fingers in the thick, silky hair at his nape, pulling him down for another kiss. He thoroughly possessed her mouth, then moved to her jaw, her chin, her throat. Her body arched uncontrollably at the hot, wet glide of his tongue across her skin.

A fiercely erotic appreciation pulsed through her. How she loved the feel of his mouth on her! And his hands, which now coursed down her body, kneading every curve, branding her with heat through the soft knit of her dress. She writhed beneath his touch, fanning the urgency between them.

He didn't spend much time on any particular area, and she fervently approved, ruled by the same driving need to connect in a larger, more full-bodied way. To rediscover. Repossess. They'd been without each other for too long. Sensual artistry could wait until this voracious, elemental hunger had been fed.

He returned to her mouth for a ravenous kiss and used both hands to mold her body to his.

She moaned at the pleasure, the rightness, the relief of reuniting with him in tight alignment from mouth to thigh. He felt harder and stronger than she remembered, yet they still fit together so well. So very, *very* well. Except she needed to twine her legs around his powerful hips. And to grind her breasts against his muscled chest. Slide her hands beneath his shirt along his sweat-dampened skin... his lean waist...his sinewy back and wide, taut shoulders. She needed all of this, and nothing would stop her from luxuriating in it.

He broke from their kiss, reared up and ran his palms around the curves of her hose-covered legs, which she'd wrapped around him. His face had beaded with sweat; his chest expanded and contracted. He pushed her dress up higher, his heated gaze following his hands. Slowly he rounded her hips, splayed his fingers around her bottom...lifted her, tilted her....

Closing his eyes, he leaned in and rocked his straining arousal against her intimate softness. She gasped and arched against the denim-clad pillar in a reflexive undulation that sent the need shooting sharply through her.

A groan rose in his throat, and he released her, only to hook his fingertips into the waistband of her hose to pull them down. She almost helped him, nearly faint with the longing to feel him push inside her, deep and hard and ultimately explosive.

But reason—cold, cruel reason—flooded back in a sickening rush. She couldn't go that far! She shouldn't have gone as far as she had! Her inner woman had somehow blinded her to practical matters, goading her beyond prudence, beyond fairness.

"Cort, stop," she cried, catching at his dark, muscled forearms. "We've got to stop. I'm not using any kind of birth control."

He stared at her with stark, sexual hunger, and she wasn't sure her words had even registered. But he finally uttered between harsh pants of breath, "Condoms. Have 'em in my wallet."

"No. That won't do. A condom could break."

He shook his head, his dark face glistening. "No, no, it won't break." He released his hold on the waistband of her panty hose...and swept the back of his fingers down in a long caress to the damp silk between her legs. Shutting his eyes, he swore in a hoarse, tremulous whisper, "I promise you, Laura, it won't."

Ripples of quicksilver sensation coursed through her loins at the slow, provocative stroke of his fingers, and she gritted her teeth against the desire to welcome him inside. A little sob lodged in her throat. She caught and held his hand. "You can't promise me that, and you know it."

Comprehension gradually stole across his face, and she knew he remembered. How could he not? They'd used condoms on such a frequent, regular basis that they'd barely given them a thought, until one had broken. He'd insisted she test for pregnancy as soon as she could get a reliable result. She had sensed such excruciating anxiety in him.

And when they'd learned she wasn't pregnant, the anxiety hadn't entirely dissipated. He'd left her a few short weeks later. She couldn't help but believe that his fear of her pregnancy had driven the first wedge between them. She understood his concern much more clearly now, of course. A baby would have meant countless complications, a moral dilemma and financial disaster.

Cort propelled himself forward and shifted to lie beside her on the sofa, pulling her into his arms and earnestly holding her gaze. "That condom was probably old when I bought it."

"We don't know that. It might have just been defective."

"A condom hasn't broken on me since, Laura. That was a single freak occurrence, and you can't stay away from sex because of it."

"I'm in the most fertile part of my cycle," she whispered.

He stared at her, digesting the information, then let out a harsh breath and tightened his arms around her. "So we'll drive to the drugstore and pick up some other form of birth control to use along with a condom. They've got all kinds, don't they? Foams and gels and so on."

"None of them are foolproof. I have friends who can testify to that. Besides, I won't use those kinds of chemicals right now. I know that might sound overly cautious, but I've been studying this subject, and...well..." She felt her face flood with color. "I'm preparing my body for pregnancy."

Again, he wordlessly stared.

To clear up any confusion that the seeming contradiction might have caused, she haltingly added, "But of course, I can't risk getting pregnant by the wrong man."

Cort wasn't sure why those softly spoken words hit him as hard as they did. They knocked the very breath out of him. They ricocheted through him like bullets off an alley wall. *The wrong man.* She couldn't make love to him, couldn't risk getting pregnant with his baby, because he was *the wrong man*.

And nothing he could say or do—no sum he could pay—would change that fact. He was, and always had been, the wrong man for her.

An almost unbearable pressure throbbed in his loins, in his head, in his heart. He wanted her so much he hurt. But he also wanted her happiness.

Gathering her to his chest, he held her close, stroked her hair and uttered into its fragrant, silky thickness, "It's okay. I don't blame you for stopping." He swallowed against a painful swelling in his throat. "Because you're right. As slim as the risk of pregnancy might be..." he clenched his teeth and finished on a whisper "...we can't take that chance."

THE HOUSE, with all its grand potential and intriguing possibilities, engaged Laura's attention for the rest of that afternoon, keeping her absorbed enough—or *almost* enough—to disregard the constant ache beneath her breastbone that had formed when Cort walked out.

If he had been angry or sullen, her emotions would have been much easier to handle. But he'd held her with such tenderness that moisture had welled again in her eyes.

After he'd released her and risen from the sofa, he told her he had work to finish at the office. He took her luggage to a bedroom, showed her the garage where his two other cars were parked and gave her the key to the one she chose. He led her to the kitchen and encouraged her to help herself to anything she wanted. His housekeeper, he'd informed her, had prepared a supper of roasted chicken, rice and vegetables, which Laura should take from the refrigerator and heat up whenever she was ready.

He wasn't sure when he himself would be back. He gave her a phone number where he could be reached. But as he spoke, he didn't look at her, or come near her. He certainly didn't touch her. And he left without a smile.

She set immediately to work, exploring the house and its graceful, stately features, absorbing the ambience of each room. She jotted down notes, sketched ideas and formulated questions to pose to Cort regarding his selections. She refused to dwell on personal matters between them, or the complicated feelings roiling within her—regret, frustration, unfulfilled longing.

But as the hours crept into late afternoon and early evening, those feelings intruded more and more. She'd wanted so much to make love to him! Was she being overly cautious in refusing to depend on a condom? She had to admit that she hadn't known one to break in fifteen years. But neither had she fully trusted one. She hadn't gone off the Pill until a few months ago...and hadn't been intimate with anyone since long before that.

How much of a risk would it actually be to make love to Cort, protected only by a condom? The answer, of course, depended on how bad the situation would be if she became pregnant by him.

We can't take that chance, he'd told her.

Although logically she knew she should be glad that he agreed with her concern, she had been unreasonably hurt by that statement. Why? Of course he didn't want a child—not now, and not from her. She thought back to what he'd said in the car: "Sex messes up a relationship based on parenthood," which she knew applied to Fletcher and her. And then, "Just like parenthood messes up a relationship based on sex." Hadn't her relationship with Cort been based on just that—sex?

He'd always been extremely cautious about not getting her pregnant. He couldn't have been more miserable after that condom had broken. And now, as a carefree, footloose bachelor, he had no reason whatsoever to change his mind about parenthood.

We can't take that chance.

Of course they couldn't! Cort didn't want to be a father to her baby, and she didn't want him to be. Her child would be raised with a steadfast, loving father—a man who would be happy and proud to play that role in his daily life.

The very idea of parenting a child with Cort provoked a sense of panic. He wreaked too much havoc on her emotions; kept her in a constant state of inner turmoil. Having a child with him would mean keeping in close contact with him, sharing every important event, knowing of the other women in his life. She would, in effect, have to play the role of his ex-wife without ever having had him as a husband.

She pressed her palm to her mouth, leaned weakly against the bare living-room wall and thanked God that she hadn't made love to him. Fletcher was the man, the only man, who could play the role of daddy without complicating her life too much.

But even as she thought it, she remembered Cort's argument that Fletcher felt something deeper for her than he admitted. If that was true, she would be subjecting Fletcher to the same kind of emotional trauma she'd just envisioned for herself with Cort...and exposing her child to an unhappy, perhaps bitter, parent.

It wasn't true, though. Fletcher felt only friendship and respect for her. They had discussed the nature of their relationship and their vision for the future many times. They would make the perfect set of parents.

She could not jeopardize that alliance by risking pregnancy with Cort. Sex for sex's sake wasn't worth the risk...no matter how much her frustrated, anguishing inner woman begged to differ.

HE HADN'T PLANNED on going to the office today. Hadn't intended to leave Laura for any extended length of time. But here he sat at 6:00 p.m., alone in his Buckhead penthouse suite, scrolling down computer screens and staring blankly at stock market reports. He'd been here all afternoon and hadn't accomplished much.

Regardless of what he did—or tried to do—the words kept running through his head: *the wrong man.*

It wasn't as if it had been a revelation. He'd known from the first time he'd seen Laura, a wide-eyed, dewy-skinned freshman whom Steffie had recruited as a housemate, that she was way out of his league. Her clothes, her speech, her graceful bearing—most of all, her naiveté—left no doubt that she'd been raised in sheltered luxury. A suburban hothouse flower.

He'd been more like the hardy weeds that sprout between the cracks of an inner-city sidewalk. He didn't belong in her garden.

He'd been deliberately distant at first. She'd paid him her first month's rent, and he'd helped her move her fine new furniture and racks of designer clothing into her room. He'd barely spoken to her, and she'd seemed to shy away from him, too. Yet she'd dazzled everyone else from the very start with her warm smile, easy friendship and striking beauty.

He'd found himself covertly watching her whenever she was around. Listening for her voice, her footsteps, whenever she wasn't. Tensing when she inadvertently ventured too near.

He probably would have managed to keep his distance if she hadn't been home alone the evening he came in with a gash above his eye from breaking up a fight at the bar where he worked. He'd had a hard time stopping the bleeding, mostly because of the shards of glass embedded in the wound. Laura had been shaken at the sight, appalled that he'd been hurt. Despite his brusque, almost rude protest, she'd followed him into the bathroom and insisted on helping him clean and bandage the cut.

That had been the first time she'd touched him. She'd pushed him down onto the commode and hovered over him, her breasts a mere whisper away from his face, her hands infinitely gentle in their work. She warmed him with her nearness, her scent, her tender caring. The beast within him prevailed, and before the night was over, he was kissing her. By the next evening, he'd taken her to bed. She became a necessity; a constant fever in his blood. A dangerous weakness.

But even during the worst of his obsession, he hadn't lost sight of reality. He barely earned enough to support Steffie and himself. He had nothing to offer a woman like Laura. She would realize it eventually, and move on.

He'd lived in dread of that day.

And then the condom had broken, and he realized how close he had come to seriously compromising her future. Was he acting honorably, making love to her night after night, when he hadn't the means to provide for her, a baby and Steffie?

The problem crystallized when her parents paid them a surprise early-morning visit and found Laura asleep in his arms. They decreed that she move out of his house and never see him again. Laura chose to defy them...even if she had to drop out of school and get a job.

Never had Cort felt so torn. How could he encourage Laura to leave the security of her parents' care, forfeit her education, throw away her future? If he allowed the beast within him to decide, he would keep her with him...even if it meant resorting to the desperate measures he'd once taken to keep Steffie and him alive.

But if he had reverted to the dark side, he would have endangered them all. On the dark side, loved ones became targets. Human collateral. He would expose no one to that danger again, regardless of the quick bucks that could be made.

He had hit a few low points in his life—when his father died slaving for pennies in a factory; when his mother had been snatched from her workplace and deported; when twelve-year-old Steffie had grown sick and hungry with no one to care for her except her sixteen-year-old brother.

Giving up Laura had been another one of those low points. *He had to leave her.* She deserved a far better life than he could provide. And Steffie needed the support he was able to give her by keeping himself unencumbered. He had no choice. He had to move far, far away from the temptation that Laura would present if he lived anywhere near her.

He hadn't been gentle when the time came to leave. He'd been crude and cruel—enough to break their bond; to make her see the futility of clinging to a relationship that could only harm them both.

Then he'd set out to make money. Serious money.

He had, at least, accomplished that goal. But he'd also learned that money wouldn't buy him everything. Or rather, every*one*.

It wouldn't buy him Laura. The years and the way he'd broken off with her had stripped away her illusions about him. She now considered him little more than a mistake in her past. She saw their affair as a "silly infatuation." At times, she hated him.

But at other times, she kissed him with a passion as fine and strong as any they'd ever shared.

Cort anchored his elbows on his desk and dragged his hands over his face. What the hell was he doing? He was obsessing over her again, just as he had in the Hays Street days.

He marveled at the irony. He had enough money to keep her in high style now, but she no longer wanted him in her life. He was still *the wrong man*.

She wanted a baby, and a man like Fletcher to father that baby. A man who had never hurt her. A man who wouldn't mess up her tidy life with blinding sexual passion. Who wouldn't mind if she indulged in a safely casual affair now and then with someone else.

As much as Cort wanted Laura, he couldn't assume the role Fletcher was willing to play. He *had* hurt her, and he wasn't sure he could repair the damage. And he wanted to mess up her tidy life with blinding sexual passion. And he couldn't tolerate the thought of her indulging in even the most casual affair with any other man.

Then, of course, came the question of fatherhood itself. If they disregarded the fact that she didn't want him in her life, took the risk of making love during the most fertile part of her cycle and the condom happened to break, how would he feel about fathering a baby?

He braced himself for the onslaught. Memories and nightmares of the times he'd been helpless to keep his family safe usually laid him low whenever the topic entered his head. Surprisingly enough, the dread didn't ambush him this time. He remembered, instead, Laura's hopeful, radiant smile as she shared her parenting plan with her friends. He remembered how she looked holding Tamika's baby—glowing with palpable happiness and maternal love. She would make a wonderful mother. He had no doubt about that. But what kind of father would *he* make?

He didn't know. He honest-to-God didn't know. That very fact generated anxiety at the thought of some sweet little kid stuck with him as a dad—for better or for worse, in sickness and in health. To Cort, a father-child relationship was binding, sacred and eternal, like a marriage vow, even more so. He would never enter into parenthood lightly.

Which meant he couldn't risk making love to her now. Because with his luck, the damn condom would break.

Darkness had descended by the time Cort drove home. He'd spent every moment of that drive firming up his resolution to keep far enough away from her to minimize temptation. He would not, under any circumstances, give in to an urge to kiss her, or hold her. Sexually speaking, she was strictly off limits.

What a major change in policy! He'd brought her here to dissuade her from her parenting plan, but also to right the wrong he'd done to her, to make her see what an important part of life she was missing by avoiding intimate relationships. Specifically, an intimate relationship *with him.*

Those goals still seemed so damn worthwhile.

With mind, body and heart engaged in fierce battle, he walked in the front door, fully intending to keep his distance from her. But then she materialized at the top of the curving staircase wearing jeans—the tight, sleek-fitting kind she'd favored back in the Hays Street days. The kind that so clearly delineated the curve of her hips, the incredible length of her legs. She wore a simple, soft white blouse tucked in at her narrow waist. She'd left her hair down, a thick, shining billow of honey-blond. And she was bare-foot...which meant she'd taken off the damn panty hose.

He stood riveted at the bottom of the stairs.

"Hi," she greeted in a soft, shy tone that reminded him of the days before he'd ever kissed her.

"Hi."

She descended the stairs slowly, as if pondering the wisdom of drawing any closer to him. "I, um, heated up the roasted chicken and vegetables. I've already eaten, but if you're hungry, I'll fix you a plate."

"No, thanks. I had a sandwich earlier."

She stopped on the last stair, which brought her eye level with him. "I've been studying the house, and can't wait to consult with you about it. I'll need to hear your ideas for the place. The things you like..." she halted, look-ing somewhat flustered, maybe because of the intensity of his stare "and the...the things you want."

Ah. The things I want. He wanted to touch her hair. Bury his hands in it. Pull her closer, breathe in her savory per-sonal fragrance. Kiss the very breath out of her.

"Tomorrow," he said. "We'll talk tomorrow."

"But I...I thought you're on a tight schedule. Unless you have something else planned for this evening, I see no rea-son we can't—"

"I need a swim," he cut in, sounding brusque and im-patient. "A long one." He hadn't intended the curtness, but the blood had begun drumming in his ears and heat in-vaded his loins. She was here, in his house, alone with him for the night—for many nights—and something about the vulnerability in her wide, brown-eyed gaze told him that if he reached for her, she wouldn't stop him from kissing her. And maybe, if he kissed her in just the right way, he could distract her from everything else—the house, her job...their *other* concerns.

He abruptly turned away from her and headed toward the back of the house, toward the heated, indoor pool. He needed vigorous physical exercise to pull him through the night.

"Cort," she called from behind him, "if you're angry with me, we probably should discuss it."

He stopped, closed his eyes in a brief grimace and turned to face her, annoyed with himself for giving her that impression. Letting out a short, toneless laugh, he assured her, "I'm not angry, Laura." He leaned his shoulder against the glossy, oak-paneled wall beneath the staircase, shoved his hands safely into his pockets and gazed at her. "Believe me, I'm not. I just feel the need for a good, strenuous workout."

Her eyes searched his, then she lifted one slender shoulder in a shrug. "Okay," she whispered.

His longing for her welled up with such force that he had to grit his teeth. He'd tried for fifteen damn years to put her out of his mind. What chance did he have of that now? Just hours ago, they'd kissed each other into a frenzy. He'd tasted her mouth, her face, her throat; he'd felt her lying beneath him again, hot and responsive, her legs wrapped around his hips, her body undulating with his.

Now he needed more than that. If he never made love to her again, if he couldn't keep her as his own, he needed at least to feel her naked against him; to bring her passionately alive in his arms. He needed it with an urgency beyond all reason.

With a sudden flash of clarity, as if God himself had supplied the answer, he knew in his heart that he was strong enough to do those things without compromising her future.

"Come with me," he breathed.

She stared blankly at him. "To swim?"

He slowly nodded.

"But I...I don't have a swimsuit."

"That's okay."

Her breath hitched in her throat, and the vulnerability deepened in her gaze. "Nothing has changed, Cort. We can't...make love."

"I know."

"Then, I don't understand." Her eyes glowed nearly golden with a sensuality he knew she couldn't help. In a wavery undertone, she asked, "What do you want?"

He drew closer, giving up the battle to resist touching her. Brushing his hand through her amber-gold tresses, he swore, "Intercourse won't enter into it."

She shut her eyes tightly and swallowed hard. A tiny pulse throbbed near her temple, and he sensed a battle raging within her.

Over the erratic clamor of his heart, he added firepower to the insurgent forces. "We'll just...play."

Her lips parted, her breathing deepened, and she opened her eyes. They'd grown sultry and dark with temptation. "But what if we go too far?"

He wove his fingers through the thick, silky locks at her nape. His other hand moved irresistibly to the sharp curve of her waist. "Have I ever lied to you? About anything?"

"No."

"Then trust me now."

She stared at him with such blazing uncertainty that he couldn't take the pressure building up within him. Gently he let go of her, pivoted and strode toward the back of the house.

Would she follow him?

Would she?

He pushed through the door of the sunporch, crossed the softly lit garden through a glassed-in walkway and unlocked the door to the pool house. If she didn't join him, he'd probably spend the whole damn night swimming laps.

He switched on the lights and adjusted them to fit his mood. Then with brisk, efficient moves, he stripped off his clothes, dropped them onto a cushioned lounge chair and dived into the heated, oblong pool. When he broke the surface, he shook the water from his eyes and turned toward the door, his body tense with the hope that she'd be there.

She wasn't.

He channeled the fierce thrum of disappointment into long, hard strokes through the water, fixing his attention on the physical effort rather than the tumultuous need storming through him. He swam lap after lap.

If it hadn't been for the slight wave of light that glistened and moved across the water, he might not have lifted his head. He might not have realized that the door had opened.

She stood there, just inside the room—silent, hesitant and so damn beautiful he could barely breathe.

Their gazes locked. He tried to force welcoming words through his constricted throat, but they got lost along the way. His muscles tensed. His body hardened into a stiff, aching arousal.

And she hadn't even taken off her clothes yet.

7

LAURA'S HEART JOCKEYED wildly about in her chest as she stood stone-still near the doorway, hugging the fluffy burgundy towels she'd brought from the nearest bathroom. Cort, too, had ceased all visible movement, having broken off his smooth, long arm strokes at the sight of her.

His eyes looked more black than midnight-blue; his wet skin darkly golden; his jet hair glossy, slicked back and dripping rivulets onto his wide, muscular shoulders.

How she wanted to taste his kiss again! To feel his hands and mouth on her. To fan his banked heat into a raging inferno. Was she wrong to act on that desire? *Intercourse won't enter into it,* he'd promised. She had no doubt he'd see to that. As much as he'd hurt her in the past, she knew she could trust his word.

We'll just...play.

Heat flushed through her, along with trepidation. She hadn't "just played" in any sexual way for years. She felt woefully unprepared. *All the more reason to go for it.*

Laura chose to ignore the objections that surfaced in the rational part of her mind as she ventured farther into the spacious, Italian-tiled room. The turquoise water in the oblong pool glistened invitingly, illuminated from within and above by softly dimmed lights. Potted tropical trees and plants thrived on all sides, interspersed with cushioned lounge chairs and small glass tables. A verdant, woodsy fragrance mingled with the steamy scent of chlorine, making her slightly high.

Or maybe it was the blood racing to her head that was causing the high. She'd almost forgotten this intoxicating rush, although she'd thrilled to it every time he'd lured her to his bed.

She had to face facts if she wanted to survive her time at Cort's house: she couldn't master this overwhelming desire simply by keeping her distance. The hours he'd stayed away had only induced greater longing, which interfered with her work. And the prospect of spending the evening beneath his roof yet apart from him seemed torturous.

Running from the desire clearly wasn't the answer. The only other option was to give in to it. To revisit the heat between Cort and her, which had taken on mythical proportions in her mind. Perhaps a dose of reality would put it into proper perspective. This time she would face the heat as an experienced woman instead of an impressionable, virginal, starry-eyed girl.

She dropped the towels onto a chaise lounge. His clothes, she noticed, had been tossed there, too. *All* the clothes he'd been wearing. Which meant he was naked.

And waiting for her.

Her pulse drummed a crazy staccato. Her temperature leaped. She had to undress. Nervously she reached to unbutton the sleeve of her blouse. His rapt gaze followed the movement of her hand, and the tension within her escalated. He hadn't said a word to her yet. He'd merely stared. Could she do this? Could she strip *completely bare* with Cort watching?

Straightening her spine, she forced her fingers back into action, fumbling with the buttons on her sleeves until one cuff fell open, then the other. That hadn't been so hard, had it?

She slid her blouse out from the waistband of her jeans and lifted her hands to the top button near her collar. And paused.

She'd been eighteen the last time he'd seen her undressed. She was now thirty-three. Friends had told her that she'd lost too much weight. She certainly wasn't as voluptuous. And though she worked out fairly frequently, she couldn't be as toned as he might remember. Her stomach clenched with anxiety. Would he be disappointed?

"Take your clothes off, Laura." His low, gruff voice echoed from across the water.

Her entire body warmed; her face flushed. She'd never suffered this kind of self-consciousness before. With other men, she hadn't felt the need to look like her teenage self. With Cort, she fervently wished she did. He'd worshiped her young body with such devout passion. She couldn't bear to see his interest, his desire, cool into indifference.

But he had to have noticed already that her body had changed. He'd felt her through the fabric of her dress. He'd seen her legs and hips sheathed in the sheerest of panty hose. He hadn't seemed disappointed then.

With her fingers poised at the top button, she caught her lip between her teeth, hesitated, then murmured, "You understand that I've...I've changed." She swallowed against a sudden dryness. "I'm not eighteen anymore."

His eyebrows gathered, his eyes narrowed. He replied in the softest of voices, "And I don't *want* an eighteen-year-old anymore."

Her face warmed with embarrassment at the topic they were discussing, and she glanced away. "I mean, it's been fifteen years since I've undressed in front of you, and um, I've lost weight. And I have a mark. Right here," she specified nervously, running her fingertip across her blue-jeaned hip. "From a burn. Hot coffee, eight years ago. It wasn't all that bad, but you can still see where—"

"Quit stalling, Laura." The gentleness of his voice didn't mask his rising impatience. "Nothing you can say is going to stop me from wanting you here, in the pool. With me. *Naked.*"

A wrenching need to comply with that directive flared within her. Holding her breath, she looked down at the small opal buttons of her blouse and worked them through the holes with clumsy fingers. Her pulse rushed in her ears, her head spun, but she unfastened every last button. She parted the edges of her blouse, and the warm, moist air billowed against her chest.

She tried not to focus on the fact that the front of her bra was fully exposed to his view, and that her cup size was now an unremarkable "B" instead of a lavishly full "C." Afraid to see his reaction, she kept her eyes on her task while she pulled the white cotton blouse halfway off.

He'd moved closer, she sensed. She braved a glance and saw that he stood waist-high in the pool near her, the ebony curls of his powerful chest glistening with water droplets, his jaw squared and hard. His gaze lingered on the swell of her breasts above the bra. "Keep going," he rasped.

Wicked heat sluiced through her veins. She recognized the dazed intensity of those midnight-dark eyes, the gruff determination of that tone. She allowed the blouse to slip down her arms and drift to the floor.

Cort felt his mouth go dry. He drank in the sight of her gently rounded cleavage; her nipples straining against the satiny white bra; the long, sleek curve of her torso tapering to an incredibly narrow waist. She tipped her head down, and her luxuriant blond hair spilled forward, hiding her breasts from him again.

She unsnapped her jeans. And lowered the zipper. A glimpse of lace-trimmed white satin mercilessly teased him. With a provocative wriggle, she pushed the tight jeans down her hips; down her long, bare, curvaceous legs. The faded denim pooled at her feet, and she stepped out of it.

She stood in only a glossy white bra and minuscule panties cut high at the hips, her lustrous hair frothing about her slender shoulders.

His blood pounded hot and fierce. She'd been ravishing as a girl—the epitome of beauty to the boy he'd been. But now she was a woman—slender, vibrant, golden and smooth. Intrinsically feminine. The epitome of beauty to the man he'd become.

Bewilderment mingled with his desire. Why had she been so unsure of herself? He frowned and studied her face, "You have to know how damn beautiful your body is...don't you, Laura?"

She stared mutely at him, as if searching his eyes for a reason to doubt. *She really hadn't known.* But how could a woman like her live for thirty-three years and not know that any man would find her body irresistibly gorgeous? What kind of fools had she been with? Or...had she not let anyone close enough to show how he felt about her naked body?

That question provoked too many strong, conflicting emotions and reminded him of things Tamika and Steffie had said. Something about Laura avoiding serious heat. Ending relationships when they got too hot.

Too hot.

The changing quality of her stare derailed him from that train of thought. Her hesitancy had waned, he noticed, and a warm, beguiling tenderness slowly dawned in its place.

"Do you know how damn beautiful *you* are, Cort Dimitri?"

Something fine and bright ignited a desire subtly different from the one that burned in his loins. He wanted to be the one, the *only* one, to show her just how much her beauty affected the male of the species, and how that beauty went far beyond the reach of time or scars. "Take off the rest of your clothes." His voice had diminished into a low rasp.

She hesitated for only a moment, then slid the bra straps down her arms. And unhooked the front clasp. Tossed the bra aside.

Hunger sliced through him, and for a wild, blazing moment, he wondered if he could do this—see her, touch her, hold her, and keep himself under control.

He would have to.

She slipped her fingers into the side lace of her panties. And paused again. "You did say we're just going to...to play, didn't you?"

His gaze traveled up her body in slow, tortured increments, past the elegant curve of her lean hips and the jaunty tilt of her high, firm breasts. When he reached her eyes, he saw that her shyness had given way to rational worry. But behind the worry burned a strikingly familiar longing, the kind that had always ignited whenever they'd begun doffing clothes.

"Yeah," he breathed. "Just play."

She nervously fingered the lace edges of her panties. "Then I...I don't really have to take these off."

The impulse struck him to climb out of the water and peel the provocative little panties down her endless legs, then run his hands over every lush, silken curve, into every valley, every cleft. "Yes, you have to take them off."

He fought to tamp down the urgency in his tone. "They'll get in my way."

Her lips parted. Her breasts rose and fell in a deeper, harder rhythm. She slid the panties down to her slim ankles and kicked the wispy satin aside.

He couldn't have been more aroused if she'd physically caressed him.

In a feverish haze, he watched her walk with her usual sensuous grace to the wide, rounded steps at the end of the pool. She was entirely naked, her skin smooth and inviting, the curls between her sleek thighs a richer, darker shade of honey than he remembered.

She was so heartbreakingly beautiful, it hurt to look at her. But he would die before he'd as much as glance away.

She descended the steps into the pool, her hand on the chrome rail, her gaze on him. The water swirled around her ankles. Then lapped at her calves. Her knees. Her waist.

Cort struggled to keep from lunging for her.

"It's heated," she murmured, a mere half-dozen arm strokes away from him. "I wasn't expecting that."

It took a moment for him to realize she meant the pool. If it weren't heated, he mused, his body temperature alone would have done the trick. The water seemed to simmer and steam around him.

She submerged herself to her breasts and glided closer. Her dusky, tea-rose nipples, a shade darker than her lips, crested through the water. The ends of her hair dipped, swirled and wafted around her.

He sank to his shoulders and drifted toward her.

She drew back, hesitant again. "Cort, I know you said we're just going to play, but..." she searched for words "...I'm not sure what you expect." Self-doubt shadowed her wide brown eyes and weakened her voice. "I...I haven't done anything like this for a very, very long time."

Though he knew he should be as concerned as her friends had been that she'd avoided intimacy, Cort felt nothing close to concern. An obstinate gladness gripped him by the throat, nearly robbing him of breath. "Do you think that fact could possibly do anything but thrill me?"

Their gazes shifted and danced with a new intensity. And he admitted to himself that what he had in mind wasn't "playing" at all. He wanted her. Desperately. And he was dead serious about it.

He lurched backward into the water, away from her, and propelled himself to the far end of the pool. Reaching beneath the diving board, he grasped the remote-control switch. With a few flicks of his thumb, the lights beneath the water and directly overhead turned off, leaving only a few silvery rays of illumination to glimmer across the surface of the pool.

"Cort?" Laura called, undoubtedly surprised by the sudden darkness.

He didn't answer. Silently he slid into the water—the dark, concealing water—and wended his way along the bottom toward her.

Let the games begin.

SHE HADN'T EXPECTED the lights to go out. The few left burning cast a dreamlike haze, like dappled moonlight glimmering off the water in some tropical lagoon. The water itself, warm as a Caribbean night against her naked skin, had gone dark and opaque.

And with a swish and ripple, Cort had vanished underwater.

Anticipation warmed Laura's stomach as she searched for signs of his approach. She felt a stirring below the surface, a subtle undercurrent, then a brushing against her thigh. She turned immediately in that direction, but heard a splash on her other side.

She whirled in time to see his head submerging again. A light pinch on her bottom startled her. With a breathless laugh, she tried to catch his arm, or leg, or whatever body part she could grab, but he was too fast and slippery. She considered launching across the pool to evade him, but she wasn't that great a swimmer...and she wanted to be well grounded for the next swim-by assault.

Another teasing pinch caught the back of her knee, sending a shiver up her leg. She lunged sideways and grabbed hold of slick skin, but he slipped from her one-handed grasp and bobbed up for air a short distance away.

"Hey," she cried, "you want a pinch? I'll give you a pinch!"

He slid beneath the silvery surface again. She held her hand and pinching fingers poised in readiness. Turning in cautious circles, she watched for vague outlines beneath the darkened water.

Hands ran up her legs in a long, winding caress. Warm sensation careened through her, and by the time she remembered her defensive-pinch strategy, he'd retreated. The water around her swirled and lapped at her suddenly sensitized breasts as she tried to imagine what would come next.

A bite nipped her inner thigh. A delicious tingle radiated upward, and her heart kicked into overdrive. All thoughts of defense fled.

So did he.

A series of bites soon nibbled at her other thigh, while his hands skimmed over her bottom...and his fingertips brushed along the sensitive crevice in a downward curve....

Her breath left her in an audible rush.

And he was gone.

She struggled to drag air into her lungs, feeling light-headed, hot and sensually charged. The next bite landed on the wickedly sensitive muscle between her thigh and pelvic bone. Her mouth opened in a silent cry. His hair floated like silky seaweed against her abdomen, and she trapped his face between her hands—this time to stop him from leaving.

He surfaced for an instant, just long enough to catch a breath, then ducked back down. A flurry of bubbles rose against her torso and breasts like a rush of fine champagne. Splayed hands gripped her backside beneath the water, and random bites rained from hip to hip, thigh to thigh.

She shut her eyes and dropped her head back, holding his taut shoulders to steady herself. The bites grew sensuous and lingering, inching ever closer to the most intimate part of her. She tilted her hips in compulsive reflex.

His rigid tongue dipped between her legs and glided upward in one hot, steady stroke. Sharp, erotic pleasure blazed through to the very core of her.

He ascended from the water like a sea god rising, and she clung to him in a breathless, sensual daze. Water streamed from his hair and down his dark, arresting face, now etched in silvery shadows. His skin radiated virile heat. His chest expanded with hard inhalations, and his fiery blue gaze sought hers.

Intensity pulsed and burned between them. He uttered not a word, not one word, but his stare said it all. *I want you. I want you!*

Her heart drummed the same need to every fiber of her being. *I want you.* She dug her hands into his wet, sinewy neck, shoulders and biceps, craving the feel of him. *I want you!*

But the limit they'd set loomed solidly between them—an obstacle they could not breach.

He ground his teeth and clutched her hips to his, trapping his arousal between them. A moan rolled from her throat, and for a moment—a wild, decadent moment—he rocked and she gyrated in hot, dangerous friction.

His grip convulsed at her hips; he released an explosive breath, and his body shifted, dislodging the velvet-smooth, steel-hard column from between them. "Ah, Laura," he rasped in a tortured whisper, a muscle throbbing near his jaw. "God*damm* it."

She reached for him, and he hungrily kissed her with deep, sexual thrusts. She strained and rubbed against his chest, her nipples raking through wet, matted curls. His hands coursed down her back and buttocks, then around to her breasts...savoring, claiming, possessing.

His arousal whispered across her thigh. She rubbed her knee along its thick, smooth length. He groaned and broke from their kiss. Gripping the underside of her thighs, he hoisted her higher, above harm's way, and folded her legs around his waist.

Which brought her breasts to his face. He took full advantage, swirling his tongue round and round until he filled his mouth; sliding his lips up slowly to catch the hardened crest. Tugging...suckling...driving her steadily into that feverish zone where nothing existed, nothing mattered, but sensation and pleasure and hot, clawing need.

Hot kisses trailed to her other breast. She closed her eyes and arched her back in sensual awe, her heavy hair dipping into the water behind her. She heard him groan as her legs locked tighter around him, and she felt the rigid muscles of his abdomen clench against her intimate feminine softness.

Her hips moved independently of her, it seemed, and she knew she'd passed the point of caution. She needed... she wanted...she moved.

With fierce pants of breath, he plunged his hand beneath the water, between his abdomen and her. And he made love to her with his fingers.

Pleasure blossomed between her legs with red-hot intensity. Every slow, forceful thrust tightened the coil of need. Water churned and lapped between them from the motion of his hand. Lights flickered behind her eyelids. Pressure built to an unbearable pitch.

And then the thrusting stopped. His fingers halted, yet remained inside, hard and long and virile. Teetering at the very edge of completion, she gasped and undulated, constricting her inner muscles to force him back into motion.

An arm banded around her writhing body, and a hoarse, urgent whisper scalded her ear. "I want to be inside you in every way I can."

Her bottom lodged against something hard. The steps. He'd settled her onto a step, where the water barely reached the underside of her thighs, his fingers still wedged inside her. His dark face wavered before her eyes, his gaze hot and fierce.

Slowly he withdrew his fingers.

Before she could even cry out at the desertion, his mouth took over. With the languorous licks...feather-light jabs... hot, suctioning swirls, pleasure blinded her. Her body arched. Her legs curled around his massive shoulders. And his tongue drove deep, launching her into hot, explosive contractions.

The force, the heat, the acute pangs of pleasure propelled her to another dimension, one she'd almost forgotten existed. Her inner woman hadn't forgotten. He'd driven her here so many, many times before.

Masterful arms gathered her close as quivering aftershocks racked her. She needed the nearness, the warmth, the kisses he feathered across her eyelids, temples and jaw. The trembling gradually decreased. The haze slowly lifted. And when reality filtered back, she realized he'd submerged them again in the warm, soothing dark water.

She nestled in his arms, curled against his chest, pressed her face to the side of his wet, muscle-corded neck. A powerful tenderness for him overcame her. "If that's what you call *playing*, Cort Dimitri," she said in a low, husky murmur, "you must throw one hell of a pool party."

He didn't answer, but tightened his arms around her. She noticed the tension in his body and the thunderous beating of his heart.

Of course. He hadn't found *his* release yet.

Languidly she slipped one arm around his neck and brushed her lips across his mouth, her breasts against his chest...and delved her hand into the water to rake her fingers up the front of his naked thigh.

His eyes shut and a small groan escaped him, but he caught her wrist and held it. "Laura," he uttered heatedly through his teeth. "As much as I'd like to keep doing this with you forever, it's time to call it quits."

"Quits?" She found his hard, pulsating arousal with her thighs and rolled it between them. He hissed in a sharp breath, and she gazed deeply into his hot, chaotic eyes. "You said you want to be inside me any way you can. There's still another way." She angled her face, sucked on his earlobe and murmured, "But we have to get out of the pool, or I'd probably drown."

With a tortured groan, he removed her arms from around his neck, slid his erection out from between her thighs and gently eased her onto her feet in the water, surprising her into silence. He looked almost angry, yet she sensed no anger in him; only frustration, desire and inexplicable conflict. "You're enough to drive a man crazy, you know that?"

With those hoarse, mystifying words, he swashed by her, climbed the steps and strode alongside the pool—wet, naked and unmistakably aroused.

Stunned at the rebuff, then distracted by the lean musculature of his powerful body, Laura watched as he grabbed a towel from the chaise lounge, vigorously rubbed his face, neck and chest dry and then slung it around his hips. She hadn't seen him naked in fifteen years. He'd only grown more Adonislike; a prime, breathtaking specimen of manhood.

"Cort?" she finally called, rousing herself from a stupor. "We can...you know...continue this upstairs, if you'd like."

"Think I'll turn in for the night," he said on his way to the door.

She gawked at his retreating back. *Turn in for the night?* "Cort, wait."

He didn't wait.

She hurried out of the pool, grabbed the remaining towel, wrapped it around herself and rushed after him. What the hell was going on? Had he been hurt somehow? Had he taken ill? She raced across the glassed-in walkway, through the house and up the stairs, heedless of her wet body and hair, or the chills racing up her spine.

She caught him in the corridor between the bedrooms. "Cort, what's wrong?" She searched his face for signs of pain or distress. "Are you okay?"

"I'm fine." He glanced down at her towel-draped form

in some surprise, although he himself wore only a towel. "You're dripping wet. And shivering."

"Oh." She glanced down at herself in mortification. "Oh, I'm sorry." She suppressed a shiver. "I didn't mean to drip on your carpet."

"The hell with the carpet." With strong, warm hands on her arms, he ushered her into a bathroom. Snatching a decorative white towel off a rack, he briskly dried her face, then squeezed the towel around random handfuls of her hair.

She watched him in growing bewilderment. She'd been ready to believe that he'd been stricken by some physical ailment, yet he looked perfectly robust. Tense and distant, but robust.

Never had he puzzled her more.

"Cort." She set a gentle, staying hand on his forearm. "I don't understand what happened. Why you...turned me down. And left me."

"*Left* you?" He seemed to object to her terminology.

"Yes, left me."

He stared at her for a long moment, the intensity again building in his gaze. Then he glanced away and tossed the damp, decorative towel aside onto a long marble-topped vanity. "We can talk about this some other time." He made a move to leave the bathroom.

She insistently blocked the doorway. "It's been an incredible evening for me, Cort. You've made me feel things that I haven't felt in a long time." Heat leaped again in his eyes, and her stomach warmed. "But I didn't want to leave it a one-way thing. I wanted to...to take care of you."

"You mean, like..." he tilted his head "...I do you, and you do me?"

Stung by the crudeness, she regarded him in uncomprehending silence. Intensity simmered just beneath his surface, and she had no idea why. "I suppose you could look at it that way."

His lips slanted almost imperceptibly. "Can't say it's not a square deal."

Anger sparked within her. "I've obviously said or done something to offend you. I don't know what it was, but you can be sure it won't happen again." She pivoted to leave the bathroom.

He caught her arm and turned her to face him. "You think you *offended* me?"

"What else could I think?"

"You can't offend me, Laura." His hands moved on her arms. His gaze played over her face. "Not when it comes to anything sexual between you and me."

Her pulse pounded; her temperature soared, and she realized that some troubling intensity simmered just beneath her surface, too. "Then what happened? Did you get tired, or bored?"

"You know damn well I didn't."

"Then tell me what. It's not fair that you should close yourself off to me when I've been so...so open to you."

He tipped her chin up and submitted her to close, hot scrutiny. "*Are* you open to me?"

She stared at him, her heart beating high in her throat. "In most ways," she whispered, thoroughly shaken and hot and wanting something beyond what he'd already given.

Cort saw the rise of desire in her gaze and felt the dangerous pull of need within him again. Dropping his fingers from her chin, he gritted his teeth in an excruciating effort to control the hunger. She was open to him in *most* ways, yes...but not all. And he wanted all.

All.

Torrid emotion stormed through him. They had reasons,

solid reasons, for not making love. He remembered only one. *She considered him the wrong man.* He could look and touch and taste; he could make her come again and again in his arms; but he couldn't have her.

That realization ate away at something vital inside of him. She had offered to tend to his sexual needs, and in keeping with their game, he should consider himself lucky. But he wanted her in a way that transcended any game he'd ever played. If she thought that mere physical release would satisfy him, she was wrong.

And he wanted her to know it.

"Talk to me, Cort," she pleaded. "Tell me why you're holding me at arm's length when we've just been so intimate. I'll respect whatever reason you have. But without understanding the situation..." she shook her head, her eyes glazed with hurt "...I won't carry on a one-sided affair."

The tension within him twisted another painful notch. She was tearing him in two. He didn't want to settle for less than all of her. The undisputed right to all of her. But if he held out for that right, he'd undoubtedly lose all chance of looking and touching and tasting. And making her come in his arms.

Her caring gaze fanned the heat he was trying to bank, and her thick tangle of wet ringlets called out to his fingers. Her scent clouded his mind—a provocative mix of chlorine, heat and woman. And the scant towel draped low across her breasts barely reached her thighs.

He looked away from her, clenched his jaw and reached deep inside for self-control. *Intercourse won't enter into it*, he'd promised. His lungs pumped hard and slow; his heart spewed liquid fire through his veins. "Okay," he rasped, turning a smoldering gaze to her. "Okay." He tangled his fingers into her billowing ringlets and cocked her face to his. "Tend to my needs then, Laura," he whispered, rubbing his thumbs beside her mouth.

And he kissed her with all the hunger that savaged his heart and body. He stripped their towels off, lifted her from the floor and perched her at the very edge of the marble vanity. Ignoring the questions in her gaze, he parted her thighs and wrapped her legs around his hips.

His arousal strained hard and erect between their bodies, planted against the curl-matted threshold of her womanhood. He braced an arm around her back and proclaimed in a torrential outpour against her ear, "I'm making love to you now."

A sound tore from her—half cry, half groan—but she didn't pull away. She didn't stop him. Cort shut his eyes, overwhelmed by the crushing weight of his promise. He couldn't have her. *He was the wrong man.* Clenching his jaw against her temple, he rocked his aching hardness against her. And in a pained rasp, he clarified, "In my mind, I'm making love to you."

Laura heard those last few qualifying words through a simmer of desire. *In his mind. Only in his mind.* Conflicting emotions rioted in her heart. Temptation to make that fantasy a reality ran the strongest.

Her throat worked in hard, dry swallows as she struggled to resist temptation. But even as she struggled, her hands swept to his taut buttocks and pulled him closer. Her fingertips kneaded muscles that bunched and flexed. Pleasure flooded her loins with every grind of his hips.

"Touch me," he breathed.

She did, in reverent awe of the power, the heat, the size. He guided her hand downward and wrapped it around the smooth, hard base of his erection. His hand then clamped over hers, and he moved in sinuous gyrations. His hardness pumped through her grip, pulsating and growing. Sensations curled in her loins from the undulating pressure against her femininity.

Heat flared. Pleasure glowed. His hand abandoned hers and climbed higher, to fist around the very top. His thrusts quickened. His muscles clenched. He groaned, stiffened and bucked.

A torrid ripple of contractions broke through both of them.

He remained absolutely still for a long moment after, his breathing ragged, his sweat-dampened face against hers. She fought for control of her own erratic breaths while the quivering in her loins subsided.

"There," he uttered almost inaudibly. "That takes care of that..." he drew back and locked her in his stare "...doesn't it?"

And though she knew he'd found release, the troubling intensity remained in his gaze.

8

NOTHING, BUT NOTHING, soothed a troubled soul as well as color schemes, fabric choices, window treatments and fine architectural detail, in Laura's opinion. Glad that her work allowed her to indulge, she rose before dawn, gathered her notebook, sketch pad and camera, and engrossed herself in the wonder of the house.

From its grandly scaled entrance doorway to its court-yard garden with an exquisite fountain to its sumptuously detailed library, the house abounded with dramatic spatial and decorative effects. Her hand almost shook as she sketched ideas, scribbled notes and snapped photographs.

She'd made her way through most of the downstairs before she realized it was almost nine-thirty. She usually started her workday with clients around eight. And Cort had not yet put in an appearance. Surely he meant to consult with her about the house. After all, he *had* insisted she break her appointment at the clinic—which would have been today, she realized with a pang of surprise—to spend the week with him.

Was he avoiding her? If so, why?

The questions renewed her emotional turmoil. Something had deeply disturbed him last night, she knew. She believed it had been the sexual limit they'd set, although he himself had agreed to the need for it. Had she been unfair to let herself revel so openly in their intimacy, when it couldn't lead to its natural conclusion? But *he* had been the one to initiate the intimate play. *He* had been the one to promise that intercourse wouldn't enter into it.

He had also been the one to honor that promise, even when she'd been ready to ignore it. Gratitude warmed her. He'd been strong, honorable and trustworthy. *He just doesn't want to get you pregnant, you nitwit!*

Which was wise. Very wise.

She, on the other hand, had been thoroughly lost to wisdom or rational thought. She'd spent years arming herself against just such mindless passion, yet within the first day she'd entered Cort's home, she'd unconditionally surrendered.

A vague fear stirred within her. It would be *so* easy to fall in love with him again.

She'd convinced herself over the years that she'd felt only a schoolgirl's infatuation for him. At the time, though, she'd believed it was love. And she'd been sure, absolutely sure, that he felt the same for her. He hadn't. He'd considered their relationship "just sex." She couldn't allow herself to forget that, or to make the same mistake twice.

Her best defense, she realized with a sinking heart, was to keep personal involvement to a minimum. She'd come too close to disaster already. *I'm making love to you now*, he'd whispered. She'd been more than willing...and he hadn't even been wearing a condom! How, how, *how* could she have been willing to take such a ridiculous risk?

Besides the risk of pregnancy, her intimacy with Cort threatened in other ways, too. Last night had led to more strained relations between them. He'd left her at her bedroom door with barely a word...and he hadn't shown his face this morning. Not a good beginning for the business she'd come to transact.

With a frustrated glance at her watch, Laura climbed the stairs, stalked down the corridor and prepared to beat on his bedroom door. She found that door open, the bed neatly made and Cort dressed in dark jeans and a black sweater, seated in an armchair with a telephone to his ear. "No, tell him the price is firm. We're not coming down a penny. And if he doesn't finalize the deal by Thursday, he might find himself in a bidding war."

Laura considered tiptoeing away to allow him to conduct his business uninterrupted, but another glance at her watch changed her mind. After all, she had canceled an important appointment to cater to his tight schedule. The least he could do now is respect *her* schedule. Bracing herself for whatever reaction he might have to seeing her this morning, she remained in the doorway of his room and briskly cleared her throat.

Cort glanced up. Met her gaze. And winked. That was it—just a slight, unsmiling wink while he listened to whoever spoke at the other end of the line.

The mere sight of his midnight-blue eyes was enough to set her pulse leaping. Dismayed at how much the slightest communication with him affected her, she returned to her own work downstairs, hoping he'd taken the hint and would soon join her.

By ten-thirty, he still hadn't.

Determined to snare his attention, she resorted to deviousness. She cooked breakfast—a particularly aromatic one that was guaranteed to draw him to the kitchen. Unless, of course, his tastes had changed drastically.

Sure enough, he soon appeared in the kitchen doorway looking morning fresh and impossibly handsome, his jet hair shining, his chiseled jaw smoothly shaven, the sleeves of his black sweater pushed up his muscled forearms. "Do I smell onions and peppers...and feta cheese?" he asked incredulously.

"And mushrooms." She tossed a glance at him from the stove. "How does an omelet sound?"

"Fantastic." He ambled closer, making her heart speed up at his nearness, and peered over her shoulder into the skillet. "You haven't salted it yet, have you?"

"Just a couple of times." She glanced at him in time to see disappointment flicker in his gaze. She elbowed him in the ribs. "No, I haven't salted it. I know you don't like much salt."

He stared at her as if she were one of the seven natural wonders of the world. His surprise made her uneasy. Maybe she shouldn't have admitted to remembering such a trivial fact after all these years. Maybe he'd make too much out of it...and start to worry that she'd never really fallen out of love with him....

He crossed his arms and leaned against the counter, studying her. "Are you going to pick the peppers out of yours?"

It was her turn to gape. She hadn't known he'd ever noticed that! "Actually, I've acquired a taste for bell peppers," she informed him, feeling marvelously mature and worldly. After a moment, though, she admitted, "But it did take almost the whole fifteen years."

They gazed at each other with smiles brimming in their eyes.

Cort couldn't say why the idea of remembering her dislike of peppers pleased him so much, or the fact that she remembered what he liked for breakfast, and how he liked it cooked.

For a moment, he'd almost felt as if she were his again.

She dished the omelet onto plates, plucked toast from the toaster and buttered both slices. She'd always been a good cook, he remembered. He'd usually refused to join in the feasts she prepared for everyone at the Hays Street house, though, unless he'd helped pay for the food. Or unless she made omelets with onions, peppers and feta cheese, which he always found a way to afford. She herself had never given the cost a thought, stocking the pantry and refrigerator with everything she knew her housemates liked.

She'd brought the Hays Street house to life with savory aromas and flavors. And colorful wildflowers. And holiday decorations on every occasion. And warm, welcoming smiles.

He'd missed her so damn bad.

The force of that feeling shook him. Why hadn't he realized it sooner? Why had he stayed away from her for fifteen years? He knew the answer, of course: he'd tried to block every conscious thought of her from his mind. He'd known he hadn't been good for her, and when he'd left, he'd meant for the break to be permanent.

And now, though he knew he could wear down her resistance to him sexually—oh yes, last night had proven that much—she'd effectively blocked him out of her heart and life with walls that seemed impenetrable.

He had to find a way inside those walls.

He had to tear them down.

The fierceness of his longing clanged warnings in his head. *When she detects serious heat in a relationship, she runs.* Steffie and Tamika had told him so. His gut told him so. If she guessed how much he wanted what she wasn't offering, she would run and never look back.

"Coffee?" she asked.

"Please."

She smiled as she poured the steaming fresh brew. She wore slim, camel-gold slacks and a soft ivory sweater with tiny buttons down the front. Her nape looked tender and sweet beneath the shining braid that lay over one shoulder. He wanted to kiss her there...and wrap his arms around her...and nibble his way down her shoulder, as he had while she'd cooked at the Hays Street house. The very thought started the wretched heat churning in his gut.

He'd made it through their intimacy last night without breaking his promise, but barely. Until he had more faith in his self-control, he couldn't let himself touch her again.

"There's no table," she remarked, glancing around the kitchen as if she'd just realized that fact. "Where do you eat?"

He hesitated. When he'd had his furniture moved into storage, he'd considered himself clever in the pieces he'd chosen to keep. "We have three choices. There's a table on the veranda off my bedroom...."

Distinct uneasiness entered her gaze, which made him wonder about her morning-after reaction to their intimacy.

"Or?" she prompted.

"A sofa and coffee table beside the fireplace in my bedroom."

"Or?"

"A reasonably uncluttered desk...in my, uh, bedroom."

She stood perfectly still for a long moment. "Are you saying that the only tablelike surfaces in the house are all in your bedroom?"

His strategic placement of furniture suddenly seemed devious. "I tend to use my room...as a private apartment," he haltingly explained. Which was, and always had been, the truth.

"How long have you lived here?"

Uneasiness glanced through him. "A few months." *Eight.* Not a good topic to expound on. She'd probably find it odd that he'd lived in a house of this size with so little furniture for eight months.

The hazy gray area between truth and deception regarding the decoration of his home made him uneasy. He'd never been less than honest with her. He didn't like having to evade issues now. But how else could he have gotten her to break her appointment at the clinic and stay with him for any length of time, if not to decorate his house? Only one minor detail had stood in his way of a perfect plan—he'd already had the house professionally decorated a few months ago. He'd simply removed all the furniture and accessories, except for a few select items, which wasn't too devious...was it?

"The courtyard pavilion has a table," he remembered.

She brightened immediately. "Great!"

He carried their coffee cups; she followed with the plates. He led her through a bedroom wing, down a wide, gleaming, oak-floored hall with graceful overhead arches and high windows, to the pavilion porch that overlooked the courtyard.

They settled at a round glass table, in wicker chairs padded with plush white cushions. He was glad for the moving company's oversight in leaving this outdoor furniture. He wasn't sure he could have stood taking Laura to his bedroom right now.

A brisk late-November breeze gusted through the two open archways and she shivered. Her shiver reminded him of last night, when she'd been wearing nothing but a damp towel and her gaze had blazed with potent invitation.

"It's brisk out here." His voice sounded hoarse. "Want to go inside?"

"No, no, this is lovely. The Palladian windows in the hall are breathtaking, and this pavilion, the courtyard, the fountain...well..." she gazed around with a vibrant smile "...it all makes me want to sing."

He lifted a eyebrow. "Do you sing?"

"No!"

They laughed, and he forced his attention to his breakfast. The omelet had been cooked and seasoned exactly to his liking. The coffee had been brewed to the perfect strength, with just the right amount of cream. And the woman seated across from him was everything beautiful, everything fine.

"You *are* planning to spend time with me today to discuss the house, aren't you?"

"I'm all yours."

She beamed. "I consider the initial consultation the most important part of the design process. It's vital that the home reflect its owner. Your home should be your personally tailored space. Your haven for peace and comfort. The place you most want to be." The ardor in her eyes and voice thoroughly captivated him. "This home exudes elegance, Cort. It breathes history. But it should also immerse you in the mood that most pleases you."

He had no doubt what mood that would be. Except he needed more than a beautifully decorated house to immerse him in it.

The moment they'd finished eating and carried their plates to the kitchen, she caught hold of his hand, like a kid at a county fair eager to see the sights. The warm spontaneity of the gesture made him smile. "Come on," she urged. "Let's get started."

Never one to turn down an opportunity, he wove his fingers through hers and savored the feel of her hand in his as she led him to the front entrance hall, out the door and down the steps.

She halted in the circular driveway, a good distance from the house. When she released his hand, he immediately missed the contact. Placing a firm, guiding hand on his arm, she turned him toward the house's fanlighted, pedimented entrance. "Now, Cort," she said from close beside him, gazing at the house with an air of solemn importance, her voice lowered in a reverent hush, "this, *this*, is your kingdom. And that entrance is its threshold—the first taste of home you'll have every time you enter. The first impression your guests will receive every time they visit. Ask yourself—what feeling do you want to evoke, to experience, when you walk through that door?"

He tried to keep his gaze on the house, as he felt sure she wanted him to do, but it wasn't easy. She was, after all, touching him, and speaking with low-key passion, and asking him what he wanted to feel, to experience, whenever he came home. Only one answer came to mind. *Her.* He wanted *her* here. The rest didn't matter.

She was gazing at him now, he realized, waiting for his reply. She was so intensely involved in the moment that if he said something profound, he could probably bring tears to her eyes.

He slanted her an indulgent glance, then looked back at the house. "Okay," he said with a nod. "I'm getting a pretty good picture of how I'd like to see the place."

She focused entirely on him, awaiting his vision. "How?"

"It might take some exterior remodeling," he warned.

"Really? Exterior work?" Her interest couldn't have been more piqued. "That will require research into the rules of historic preservation. Since this neighborhood is on the historic register, rules are very strict." Her curiosity fairly blazed. "But we can certainly try. What's your idea?"

He regarded the house with deep contemplation again, rubbing his chin. "A pirate ship, I think," he mused. "Yeah...a pirate ship. We can build up the front to look like its bow. You know, put a masthead above the door.

Raise a pole on the roof, and fly a skull and crossbones from it." He glanced at her. "What do you think?"

She slugged him in the arm. Hard. "Damn you, Cort! I thought you were going to be serious about this."

"Aw, Laura, I'm trying, but I'm not the one with artistic vision about these things. A house is a house to me. Sure, this is a damn nice one, but—"

"Don't you care how this project turns out? Doesn't it matter if you like what I do with your home?"

He immediately sobered at the hint of hurt in her gaze. "Of course it matters. I wouldn't have hired you if it didn't."

"But I can't do a good job without your input. The most important part of decorating a home is incorporating the tastes and personality of its owner."

"Doesn't pleasing the owner count for anything?"

"Well, yes, of course, but—"

"You know how you can please me?"

She cast him a wary glance, as if she was afraid to ask. "How?"

Gripping her shoulders, he turned her to face the house, his gaze aimed at the entrance. "I want you to see this as *your* house, Laura. *Your* haven. Your personally tailored space. Do whatever you want with it. Cater to your artistic spirit." His gaze shifted from the house and locked with hers. Vehemently he whispered, "Make it the place you most want it to be."

Her gaze intensified. Searching, delving into his...yet somehow growing more unreadable. He sensed heat, but it could be his heat. He sensed surprise, and uncertainty. And...alarm?

He'd said too much. Gone too far. "I trust your instincts implicitly," he said, striving for damage control. "You took the ramshackle old house on Hays Street and made it into a home. A warm, comfortable home. If you do that now, Laura, you can't fail to please me."

He lapsed into tense silence. Held his breath. Searched her eyes.

A sheen slowly welled there. "Thank you," she whispered. She looked deeply honored and emotionally moved. Pressing her lips together, she subdued the threat of tears and smiled. "I'll do my very best for you," she solemnly swore.

And before he could manage another breath, she walked back to the house without so much as a backward glance at him, lost in thought and glowing with creativity.

The door closed behind her. Cort shook himself out of a trance, then ruefully cocked his head. Perhaps he'd made a mistake. Now she didn't need him around at all. He'd blown his chance to work with her, side by side, possibly for days.

Nice work, genius.

Before he reached the house, she reappeared at the door. "Don't think you're off the hook." Her voice lilted with a gentle chiding. "If I'm going to 'cater to my artistic spirit,' I'll need your input to inspire me."

He twisted his mouth in mock dismay, purely for dramatic effect. He couldn't remember ever feeling quite this happy, and for no clear-cut reason.

In a remarkable show of mercy, she didn't try to force him into making selections of wallpaper, fabric and carpet, as the previous decorator had. She did, however, shepherd him from room to room, asking what he liked best, and how he intended to use the room, and whether its current layout seemed less than perfect.

She had him survey each area from a variety of angles, directing his attention to certain features. She coaxed him into feeling samples of fabrics and describing what each brought to mind. They sprawled out on the plush, Oriental carpet in the library with stacks of books and magazines, and she had him point to scenes that caught his eye. She asked whimsical questions that seemed irrelevant—what were his favorite scenes in movies, the most intriguing places he'd visited, the childhood memories he considered the happiest.

He humored her. And teased. And forced her into sharing her opinions, memories and reactions. They laughed themselves silly. She slugged him a few times. He caught her in the middle of a mock scolding and kissed her.

She threaded her fingers through his hair. He pulled her closer. The kiss turned from playful to erotic. He pressed her down against the plush library carpet, and their kisses grew hungry. Ravenous. He ran his hands beneath her clothes.

The beast in him took over. He unbuttoned her sweater; unzipped her slacks. The urgency burned within him. He wanted her naked again...and to be inside her, deep inside, in any way he could....

Before he'd managed to strip off even the first piece of clothing, a distraction came in the form of a phone call. The answering machine, which he'd hooked up to the intercom to screen for important calls, blared a familiar masculine voice throughout the house.

"Laura, it's me. Fletcher."

She stiffened in Cort's arms.

"I really need to talk to you," boomed the annoyingly urgent voice, "so call me as soon as you can."

Laura uttered a soft cry, pushed away from Cort and sat up, fumbling to readjust her clothing. "I have to call him. It sounds like something's wrong."

Cort cursed beneath his breath and helped her button her sweater.

Zipping her slacks, Laura rushed from the library, feeling hot and disoriented, and highly aware that the call had probably saved her from herself. She'd been lost again; lost in the heat and mindless desire that Cort provoked so easily. Would she have stopped before going too far? Would Cort have diverted their passion in some creative way, as he had last night?

One thing she knew for sure: they couldn't carry on like this for long. She had to either be strong and keep him at a safe distance, or...or what? Resort to the use of condoms and pray they wouldn't break?

The chance of a defect is slim, she told herself. *Millions of people rely on condoms every day.* But one *had* broken on them before, and scared the joy right out of their relationship. An accident like that would certainly scare her now. Too much!

She was already reading profound emotion into things he said and did. The warmth she'd thought lost forever had somehow blazed back to life, and not only because of their sexual chemistry. Or so she could too easily convince herself....

She closed her bedroom door, drew her calling card out of her purse and placed a call to Fletcher from the bedside phone. She had to be strong enough to resist Cort, as well as her own inclination to read meaning into his casually caring ways. She had to be smart enough to guard her heart and control her own future.

"Fletcher," she said into the receiver, relieved to hear his voice again. He was part of the sane, orderly world she'd left behind, and the sane, orderly future she had carefully planned. She desperately needed a reminder of both right now. "Is something wrong?"

"Laura, I've been worried sick about you. Are you okay?"

"Of course I am. Why wouldn't I be?"

"I've been thinking about what you said. About Cort's motivation. Maybe I was wrong to encourage you to go. Has he tried anything with you? Does he expect you to sleep with him?"

She sank slowly onto the bed, stunned by the questions. Her first impulse was to reprimand him for talking about Cort that way. Cort didn't deserve the disrespect and suspicion that those questions implied. *Has he tried anything with you. Does he expect you to sleep with him.* Her very heart flinched. But how could she admonish Fletcher when she herself had been the one to first question Cort's motivation?

"Laura? Oh no...I *was* wrong to send you, wasn't I?"

"No, Fletcher. I'm glad I'm here. Things are going fine. There's no need for you to worry."

"Are you telling me he's been keeping it strictly business?" He let out a dry laugh. "I find that hard to believe."

Sharp, conflicting emotions tore at her. The strongest was indignation. How dare he pursue the issue when she'd told him not to worry? How dare he question Cort's behavior in his own home? At the same time, she knew he was asking out of concern for her, and maybe guilt that he had pushed her into an awkward situation. She was being unfair to Cort and to Fletcher by not making it clear that her relationship with Cort had changed.

"Uh, Fletcher..." Laura cleared her throat, feeling inexplicably awkward. Why should she hesitate to tell Fletcher the truth? They prided themselves on their honest, open relationship. "You don't have to worry about what Cort does in that respect. *I'm* not worried." *Liar!* "What I mean is—" What *did* she mean? "Cort and I have reached a personal understanding. And because of it, we've become... closer."

"Closer? Does that mean you're sleeping with him?"

Anger stirred in her, and she bit back a sharp reply. But then confusion set in. Didn't Fletcher have the right to ask her that? As the chosen father of her future baby—her parenting partner—perhaps he *did* have a moral right. He wouldn't want her conceiving another man's baby if he planned to claim paternity. "No," she finally answered. "I'm not sleeping with him."

"You hesitated," he charged. "Why?"

"Fletcher! Do you think I'm lying?"

"No, not lying," he said, clearly miserable. "I know you wouldn't lie. But there's something you're not telling me."

"I'm not sleeping with him, and he's not behaving in an inappropriate manner. What else do you need to know?"

A few beats of uncomfortable silence passed. "I saw the video."

She frowned. "Pardon me?"

"B.J. gave me the computer disk with pictures from the Hays Street house. I knew you and Cort were a couple before I moved in, but you didn't seem especially close while I was there. Not like in those pictures."

Laura immediately realized why. Fletcher had moved in after the condom crisis; her relationship with Cort fell into two distinct categories—before and after the crisis. "What do those pictures have to do with anything, Fletcher?"

"You were all over each other. Constantly. And the way you looked at him... The way you kissed him..." A sick, anxious feeling wormed its way into Laura's stomach. Fletcher was upset. Far too upset. He'd never spoken to her with such bleak emotion. "You were so damn in love with him."

A pang went through her. "So what?" She clutched the phone tightly. "What does that matter now?"

"Are you still in love with him?"

"No."

"Can you swear to that, Laura? We're supposed to have a baby together, you and I. Raise a child. Start a family. What's going to happen to us if you're with Cort?"

"I won't be with Cort!"

"I wish I could believe that." His voice broke, and she pressed her hand to her heart, terribly afraid that he was fighting tears. "Those pictures explained a lot." He sounded so forlorn, she could have wept. "I've been with you for fifteen years. Fifteen years, Laura! While Cort was off doing his own thing, I was there for you."

"Fletcher." She forced words out through a constricted throat. "I don't believe you've been completely honest with me."

"I've always been honest with you."

"You swore it wouldn't disrupt our relationship if either of us had an affair."

"You've had affairs here and there. Did I ever object? No. But this is more than an affair, Laura, even if you haven't slept with him in fifteen years. Can't you see that?"

She *did* see it. And it frightened her. The passionate unhappiness in Fletcher's voice frightened her, too. She felt as if all her security, all her comfortable assumptions, were collapsing around her like a house of cards. "You said you felt only friendship for me."

Silence stretched tautly between them.

"Maybe I haven't been completely honest with myself about you," he said in a tight, pained whisper.

She understood then what he was feeling, and her heart bled for him. She'd suffered the same kind of pain. And because she cared so much about him—loved him, in a way—she was tempted to say anything, promise him anything, to make him feel better. But she couldn't, because false hope would only end up hurting him more. She didn't love him the way he deserved to be loved.

And for the first time, after years of struggling to reconcile the caring and warmth of a close relationship with the seeming coldness of goodbye, she clearly understood the dynamics of a one-sided love.

She finally understood how Cort must have felt when he'd left her.

CORT TRIED TO BIDE his time by opening the mail, but soon gave up. He couldn't focus on any one piece long enough to make sense of it. He considered taking a quick swim, just to work off the excess energy, but the memories awaiting him at the pool were too fresh and evocative for him to handle. Besides, if something was wrong, as Laura had suspected when Fletcher first called, he wanted to be immediately available for her.

What in the hell were they talking about for this long, anyway? Glancing at his watch as he paced across his bedroom, he realized that almost an hour had passed since she'd closed herself up in the guest bedroom.

He struggled to keep his mind open and his attitude reasonable. Fletcher was, after all, her business partner. They probably had a lot to discuss. Cort's flare of annoyance at the interruption had been selfish and illogical. He actually should be grateful for the interruption, considering the fact that his desire for Laura had pushed him beyond the boundaries of caution. His self-control had worn too thin. He should be damn glad that Fletcher had called.

But he wasn't.

He saw no sense in hiding from the truth—he resented Fletcher's relationship with her, his influence over her and the fact that he had pulled her away from Cort's arms. Fletcher's role in her life would only expand in scope and importance, while Cort's would be virtually over when she left his house.

He felt wronged, yet he knew that no one had wronged him. He felt abandoned, yet she was still here, and responsive to him. He felt sick with jealousy over a guy who had probably never kissed her, probably never held her, and certainly never made love to her. A guy who cowered behind the role of friend.

But *that* guy had a future with her. He would share profoundly intimate moments and lifelong ties with her.

Cort paced, plowed his fingers through his hair and cursed. He wanted her with a soul-deep craving that grew worse day by day. He'd been telling himself it was the same old sexual obsession he'd fallen victim to years ago, just a physical reaction to her beauty. But how could that account for it, when his sexual release last night had left him feeling empty and deprived? The warmth and laughter they'd shared today had touched him far more deeply. Yet the warmth and laughter had somehow heightened his need for her kiss, her touch, her body.

If he didn't make love to her soon, he just might die.

He was caught in a vicious cycle. Trapped.

He had to talk to her about it. He had to tell her how he felt, as confused and desperate as it might sound. Steffie and Tamika's warnings—and Laura's own insistence that she felt nothing for him but sexual desire—had stopped him long enough. The situation called for honesty. Complete, unabridged honesty.

And there was no time like the present. Relieved in some part by the decision itself, he crossed the hall and raised his fist to rap on the door. He found it slightly ajar. "Laura?"

She didn't answer.

Wondering if she'd slipped out without him noticing, he

pushed the door open. He found her sitting in the window seat, gazing out the large bay window, her legs folded beneath her. The late-afternoon sun cast long shadows over the gardens below and turned her hair to molten gold.

"Laura?" He ambled closer and realized from her pale, somber face that something was wrong. Very wrong. His heart lurched, and he sat on the window seat beside her. "Laura, what happened?"

It took a while, but her gaze eventually met his. "Our plans have changed." Her eyes looked darker than usual and red-rimmed. Almost...mournful. "Mine and Fletcher's"

Cort stared at her, too stunned to fully process the information; too wary of jumping to false conclusions to formulate any at all. "Which plans?"

She looked away from him again and stared out through the window. "We won't be merging our businesses, or working together. Or...having a baby."

The news, which he'd been hoping for, praying for, had hit too suddenly for him to grasp. "Why?"

Color warmed her face, and she glanced down at her tightly clasped hands. "Because you were right. He hasn't been completely honest about his feelings for me. He wants..." her voice shook, so she resorted to a whisper "...more than I can give."

A heavy silence settled around them while she marshaled her self-control and he struggled to understand exactly what had happened. "He told you this?"

"In his own way."

Foreboding curled through him.

Her desolate gaze appealed to his for understanding, or maybe comfort. "I...I can't reciprocate his feelings, but I do care about him. Very much. Too much to keep hurting him. I think it's better for both of us to...to go our separate ways."

Cort stared at her with such a volatile mix of emotions he couldn't find his voice to comment. The relief of having his rival gone from the picture was grotesquely overshadowed by a grim, inescapable truth. She'd axed the guy from her life *because he'd fallen in love with her*.

And he'd made the mistake, the fatal error, of telling her so.

9

HE NEEDED TO GET them the hell out of the house. He needed distraction—noise, people, music, food. He also needed to talk to her, to understand what she was feeling and thinking. And to hold her in his arms, at least for a while tonight. The safest, surest way to do all those things was over dinner and, afterward, on some intimate little dance floor.

"I'm taking you out tonight." He didn't bother to ask. He knew she wouldn't want to go.

He was right—she didn't. She said she preferred to work on wall-covering selections. As a second line of defense, she added that she'd brought nothing to wear for an evening out.

Cort called an upscale neighborhood boutique, and within an hour, the store had delivered a selection of cocktail dresses. Laura was stunned by the delivery, awed by the styles and intimidated by the prices. "I can't afford any of these, and I won't have you buying me clothes."

"Pick one, or I'll buy them all. Better yet, try them on, and *I'll* pick one."

She'd been too despondent to oppose him for long. He chose a dress of soft, black chiffon that molded to her hips and swirled in semisheer layers around her thighs, and left her long, shapely back virtually bare. She wore high heels, and small diamonds in her ears. She'd caught her thick, lustrous hair behind one ear with a decorative comb, but otherwise left her golden tresses flowing and free.

She looked elegant. Sexy. Impossibly beautiful.

And sad.

He took her to Thea's place, a small midtown restaurant and piano bar. Thea herself wasn't there when they arrived but her smiling, vivacious granddaughter Helena led them to Cort's usual table in a secluded, gardenlike setting. Savory aromas of roasted meat, garlic, lemon and olives scented the air.

Nothing soothed a troubled soul quite like a fine Greek meal, a bottle of ouzo, and soft music, to Cort's way of thinking. Laura preferred wine to the strong, anise-flavored liqueur, so he filled her glass with fragrant Chardonnay.

"I have no idea what most of these dishes are," she remarked, studying the menu. "It's all Greek to me."

He smiled at the joke. At least she *was* trying to lighten the mood. He ordered a selection of his favorites for her to try—yuvetsi, a lamb dish with a delectable tomato sauce; moussaka, a layering of eggplant, beef and potatoes; souvlaki, delicately seasoned pork; grilled garlic shrimp; salads with Kalamata olives, hot peppers and feta cheese; and warm, fresh bread.

The food, as always, was excellent. Laura exclaimed a number of times in earnest appreciation, and surprised him by actually eating a fair portion. But he had only to look in her eyes to know that her heart was heavy.

When the dishes were cleared away, he leaned forward, rested his forearms on the table and held her hands warmly in his. "Thank you for coming out with me tonight. I thought it would do us both good to get away."

She gave him a slight, rueful smile. "I'm sorry. I know I'm not very good company."

You're the only company I want. He couldn't say that, though. She might take it as a casual compliment, or she might realize how much he meant it. And then he would be cut out of her life, as Fletcher had been. "Just talk to me, Laura."

She stared at him, as if too mired in her misery to know where to begin. He suspected that her sorrow over Fletcher hurt her nearly as much as her ruined plans for having a baby.

He would give her time to broach the subject of her foiled parenthood plan if and when she was ready. The subject of Fletcher, however, needed to be dealt with immediately. "You're feeling bad about Fletcher, aren't you?" he prompted.

"Of course. I hurt him. And our friendship will never be the same."

"The same as what?"

"The same as...well, as I thought it had been for all those years. But I guess I'd been seeing only one side of it." A puzzled frown gathered in her eyes. "You knew the truth before I did. How?"

He shook his head, at a loss for an answer. How to explain his ultrasensitive awareness of other men's interest in her? And the possessiveness that gripped him whenever he detected it. Right now, for instance, half the men in the place had eyes for her. He was fine with that, as long as they kept a respectful distance...and their fantasies remained just fantasies. "A hunch, I guess."

"I'm sorry I didn't believe you sooner." She closed her eyes and whispered with anguish, "I hate to think of what could have happened if I'd kept that appointment. If I had..." she paused, her lips briefly compressed "...conceived his baby."

Cort hated to think of it, too.

"I would have made Fletcher miserable," she said. "He was already so upset with me."

"Why?"

A blush slowly rose in her face. "He thought that we— that you and I..." She hesitated, as if unsure of how to word it.

"—are having an affair?"

"Not exactly. He seemed to believe me when I said we aren't sleeping together. I felt he had the right to be assured of that particular fact, in light of our parenting plan."

Cort tensed at the idea that she'd been obliged to share any information at all about their intimate relationship with Fletcher. He wanted no other man to have that personal claim on her. He wanted his sexual bond with her to be no one else's business; to be held sacred by one and all. Inviolate. *Let no man put asunder.* "Then why was he upset?"

"He thinks that I..." she glanced away from him, then returned with an uneasy gaze "...that I'm in love with you."

Cort went very still, every system in his body slowing to a near halt. "And how did you respond to that?"

"I told him he was mistaken."

He tried very hard not to take it personally. But it wasn't easy. The confusion, the need, the restless torment swelled into a painful pressure within his chest. She wasn't in love with him. No news there. Yet it hurt to hear her say it.

The silence between them grew too tense, and he forced himself to relinquish her hands. The contact had become too much for him. Then again, not enough. He wanted to sweep her out of the chair, take her home to his bed and make love to her until she needed him as much as he needed her.

But she would leave him if she knew the feelings raging inside of him, so he said and did nothing.

Laura wrapped her fingers around her wineglass and stared into its shimmery pale depths, relieved that Cort had let go of her hands. His warm touch and probing gaze were playing tricks with her heart again. She could so easily believe that he felt more for her than sexual attraction, or concern, or friendship. But she'd allowed herself to fall victim to the same seductive delusion fifteen years ago. She couldn't tolerate the heartbreak again. She wasn't sure if she could survive it this time.

Feeling the need to change the subject, she said with perhaps a little too much formality, "I suppose we should discuss the business ramifications of mine and Fletcher's breakup. Since we won't be combining our businesses or incorporating, I'm assuming you'll withdraw your investment offer."

His dark blue gaze played across her face, somehow reminding her of the hot, sweet intimacies they'd shared last night; reminding her that it wasn't all business between them. "I'll tailor my offer to fit the new circumstances." His tone was as formal as hers. "I'll call Fletcher tomorrow, or whenever you feel that I should, and adjust the amount and the terms of our agreement. And you and I can discuss my investment in *your* business at your convenience."

Relief washed through her. Hurting Fletcher emotionally had been bad enough, but depriving him of the financial backing that meant so much to him had weighed heavily on her conscience. At least he would still have the opportunity to expand his business.

She, on the other hand, wasn't too sure about accepting Cort's money. Her defense system fairly screamed at her to finish the decorating job and get the hell out of his life.

"Ah, Cortland! Helena told me you were here." A tall, handsome woman appeared at their table, beaming a welcoming smile at Cort. Touches of silver gleamed in her well-coiffed dark hair, and rubies glimmered at her wrists, ears and throat. "It's been months since you've been in."

"Thea." Cort rose from his chair, hugged her and introduced her to Laura as the owner of the best *kouzzina* in Atlanta.

Laura complimented her on the food and the elegant decor, then cocked a curious eyebrow at Cort. *"Cortland?"*

"Thea's the only one who gets away with that," he warned, "and only because I have no choice. She saved my life. It would be rude of me to kill her."

Thea laughed and pressed him back down into his seat with an affectionate hand on his broad shoulder. "I didn't save his life," she told Laura. "I helped him fill out paperwork and tutored him with his history lessons."

"She helped me pass my test for citizenship when I was just a punk off the street. And she gave me a job when no one else would. Believe me, Thea...you saved my life."

"Bah! You paid me back many times over." She turned a shining gaze to Laura. "Three years ago, my husband was sick, and our old restaurant was falling down around me. Between repair bills and medical bills, I couldn't even afford to hire help to keep the business open. Next thing I know, Cort comes back to the old neighborhood for a visit and buys us this place."

"I didn't buy you this place, Thea. I invested in your business. There's a difference. I'm making more and more money from it every day."

"Praise be to God." To Laura, she said, "He's always had a good heart, even when he was a punk." With a wink and smile, she said, "Have dessert. It's on me. The baklava was baked fresh today." She turned to leave their table, halted, then faced Cort again. Her expression, Laura noticed, had inexplicably sobered. "By the way, Anatole was here for dinner a few weeks ago. He said that if I see you, I should send his regards."

Although Cort's expression didn't actually change, Laura sensed tension stealing over him. "If you see him again," he replied pleasantly enough, "please don't send him mine."

Thea's eyes flashed with approval. With another smile for Laura, she caught their waiter on his way past the table and asked him to bring coffee and dessert. She then glided off to greet other customers.

Laura realized how little she really knew about Cort and all the years he'd spent without her. "Who's Anatole?"

"A man I used to work for." The tension remained visible in the taut planes and angles of his rugged face. Though he looked strikingly elegant in a dark Brioni suit, ivory shirt and silk gray tie, she sensed a raw, savage power now leashed at the ready.

What, she wondered, had incited his tension? Laura felt that he was closing her out, as he did every time his past was mentioned. "You asked me to open up to you, Cort, and I have. Now it's your turn to talk to me. Tell me about Anatole."

He stared at her for a long, tense, assessing moment. "Okay." His tone, quiet yet harsh, sent a shiver up her arms. "Anatole owned a number of businesses in the neighborhood where Steffie and I rented a room when we were kids. When I got off work from my job at Thea's, I stole cars for Anatole. And ran numbers. Collected overdue debts for his loan sharks and bookies."

Laura tried not to flinch or show her shock and dismay. She hadn't known! Wouldn't have believed it if he himself hadn't told her. Her blood curdled at the thought of the danger and corruption he'd faced...and at such a young, vulnerable age.

The hardness in his eyes and jaw grew more pronounced. "You understand now how naive you were back in our Hays Street days, don't you, Laura? You looked at me with such admiration and trust, as if I could do no wrong." He let out a harsh breath. "I felt like a damn fraud."

A cry of protest broke from her. "You did what you had to do to keep you and Steffie alive. Call me naive, but I can't hold that against you. Steffie told me how your father died when you were both so young, and how little money there was, and that your mother couldn't qualify for citizenship. And then, for her to be snatched away from you without warning..."

"It was very hard on Steffie." He said it as if he himself had not been affected. But dark, pain-filled memories lurked in his hooded gaze, whether he wanted her to see them or not. "It might not have been as much of a shock if we had grown up on the streets," he continued almost reluctantly, as if she'd somehow compelled him. "But my mother had worked as a housekeeper for a wealthy family for a few years, and we'd gotten used to a fairly decent life. She lost that job suddenly—the lady of the house was displeased by something. We never knew what. The only place my mother could find work was in a rough, inner-city neighborhood. That's where the INS agents caught her in a raid."

Laura's heart went out to him and his family, but she knew he would detest her sympathy. A waiter set cups of aromatic coffee and plates of flaky, layered, honey-fragrant pastries in front of them. Cort bent his attention to his coffee, the heavy gold and black-sapphire ring on his hand glinting in the candlelight as he reached for the cream.

"Is that when you began working for Anatole—when your mother was deported?"

"Soon after the cash under the mattress ran out." His mouth thinned in a sardonic twist. "Anatole paid well."

"How did you ever manage to get away from that life?"

He held her in a dark, steadfast, piercing gaze. "How do you know that I did?" She stared at him, unsure of what he meant. "After all, how would a backstreet hood like me end up with twenty-some million dollars?"

His insinuation hit home, and she tightened her mouth in anger. "Give me more credit than that. I know you, Cort Dimitri. At the age of twenty-two, you wouldn't eat lunch meat from your own refrigerator unless you'd paid for it. You wouldn't buy beer for your underage friends who'd tried dozens of times to bribe you. You wouldn't allow illegal drugs in your house, and God help Steffie if she associated with anyone who used them. I will never believe you made your fortune in any unethical way."

A muscle moved in his cheek—the start of a smile, maybe—but his gaze remained hard and unreadable. "You're still very naive." A tense silence drew out between them, but he finally confided in a soft, gruff voice, "The last job I did for Anatole was a collections run. Gambling debts. I watched my older, more experienced cohort shatter a man's kneecaps."

Horror washed through Laura. A hazy recollection returned to her—of Cort hot and trembling in the dead of night, hoarse gasps about bloody knees and baseball bats uttered in the throes of his nightmare.

She reached across the table and covered his dark, strong, beautiful hands with hers, hurting for him in a vague, helpless way. She couldn't think of how to express her wish that she could have saved him from all that horror without embarrassing him into silence. "How did you get away from Anatole?"

He shrugged. "I turned in my notice." He smiled, and she didn't believe she'd ever seen a smile more devoid of humor. "He didn't accept it very graciously. He threatened to put Steffie to work in one of his, uh, *houses*." He raised his coffee to his mouth, but set it back down without drinking. "She was thirteen at the time."

Laura stared at him, appalled. She had no doubt what kind of house he'd meant. "You couldn't have been more than seventeen yourself. What did you do?"

"I left town with her. We caught a bus. Went to a friend of Thea's. Eugene Petrandis, in Athens."

"Athens, Georgia?" A silly question, she immediately realized. She had, after all, met him there. Lived with him there.

"Damn sure wasn't Athens, Greece. Not that I hadn't thought of going there. But we had no money for airfare, no passports and no idea of how to get in touch with my mother. Eugene finally found a way to reach her in Greece, but it took time." He leaned back in his chair and shrugged. "Anyway, as you might remember, I worked in Gene's bar for the next five years."

"Gene," she said with a reminiscent smile. She remembered the quiet, white-haired man with the walruslike mustache from his few brief visits to the house.

"He and Thea made all the difference in my life." The hardness, she noticed, had left Cort's eyes. "He lent me money for the down payment on the Hays Street house and cosigned the loan. And when I left Athens, he and a few other investors backed me financially in the idea I had for a sports bar."

"Where is he now?"

"He passed away six years ago. When he died, he left me his share of all the sports bars we'd opened together." Cort shook his head, his stare unfocused. "I wish like hell he could have been around to see the price those bars brought as a national chain. He would have gotten such a damn kick out of it."

Her throat constricted at the sorrow in his gaze. "I'm sorry you lost him. And I'm sorry about your mother's death, too. She was a lovely woman. I remember Steffie flying to Greece last year for her funeral. I wish I could have gone."

With a little jolt of surprise, Cort remembered Steffie mentioning that Laura had met their mother when she'd returned to the States for brief stays—after she'd married a fairly well-to-do Greek businessman. Steffie had already graduated from college by that time, and Cort himself had been too immersed in his fledgling businesses to see his mother as much as he'd wanted to. The fact that Laura had met her and remembered her with fondness touched him deeply.

But what touched him even more was the realization that he'd told Laura the sordid truth about his past—a truth that not even Steffie fully knew about—and the warmth hadn't left her gaze. He hadn't been able to bluff her into thinking the worst about him, either. Of course, he couldn't make too much out of her warm regard for him. That warmth had its limit.

And that limit grated on him more than ever.

Because, over the course of their conversation, a very basic truth had crystallized in his heart. He loved her. He loved her now, and he'd loved her then, from the very first time she'd touched him.

If he hadn't loved her, he wouldn't have let her go. He would have defied her parents and their ultimatum, which would have forced her to drop out of college. He would have shackled her to him with marriage, babies and obligations. And by the time she realized that she didn't really love him, that she had nothing in common with a penniless thug from the wrong side of town, she couldn't have found it in her heart to leave him.

But he *had* loved her, even if he hadn't allowed himself to call it that. So he'd let her go. He'd let her find her rightful future as a free, unencumbered, college-educated woman.

And time had proven him right. She'd realized she hadn't really loved him at all.

The honorable thing now would be to finish his business transactions with her and let her go back to her life. But he wasn't a saint, or a Boy Scout, or even a particularly good man.

He wanted her. The years he'd spent without her had been etched in stark black and white, and more often, gray. She brought bright, vivid color to his life. Softness. Sweetness. She made his heart sing, his blood race. She lit a soul-stirring passion in him that no one else ever had or ever could. He wouldn't let her go again—not until she made it very clear that she was finished with him, once and for all.

He hoped to delay that eventuality for as long as humanly possible. Which meant he couldn't, under any circumstances, make the same mistake Fletcher had.

He tried to force a smile, but knew he didn't quite manage it. His need to touch her, to hold her, had grown too great. Rising from his chair, he murmured, "Let's dance."

She rose and took his hand. As he ushered her through the crowded room toward the dance floor, a young couple stood up to leave from a table in front of them. The woman held an infant wrapped in blankets.

Cort wasn't at all surprised when Laura stopped beside

her, murmuring in soft, lilting tones. The woman peeled back the blankets and showed her the baby. Laura gazed with such tenderness and awe and palpable longing that something powerful moved in Cort's chest. The couple soon ambled past them, and Laura's wistful gaze followed.

A treacherous yearning squeezed Cort breathless. He longed to banish the wistfulness from her eyes; to infuse her with that tender, loving glow. To be a part of that glow. To cause it, to bask in it. He wanted to give her everything—*everything*—she desired.

The moment they reached the small, vacant dance floor, he pulled her into his arms, solidly against him, with a little more force than was strictly civilized. She didn't seem to mind. Her arms went around him. Her body molded to his. He buried his face in her golden hair, inhaled its misty-rose fragrance and shut his eyes. They swayed to the rich, soft piano music in the same way they'd always danced— a slow, rhythmic shifting of their bodies in subtle, sensual synchrony.

He hungered for her.

And he hungered for the life they could have together.

"Laura," he breathed, his hand coursing down the velvet-smooth contours of her naked back. "Why do you want a baby so much?"

She didn't answer at first, and he lifted his head to gaze down into her face. Sadness glistened in her honey-brown eyes. "That's not an easy question to answer."

"Try."

For a reason she didn't quite understand, Laura felt too emotionally vulnerable right now to talk about her quashed dreams. But the compassion in his gaze, the caring warmth of his embrace, the caress of his strong, familiar hand, summoned the words from deep inside of her.

"I want someone of my own. Someone I can love, and who will love me...always." Her throat closed, and she choked out a laugh at her own silliness. "I want to be a team mom. A room mother. Santa Claus. The Easter Bunny. The tooth fairy!" She blinked away a foolish prickling behind her eyelids and pressed a trembling smile against the side of his neck. "Most of all, I want to be the one he's calling when he wants his mama."

She lapsed into throat-aching silence.

He gathered her closer, his arms strong and comforting. The song ended. Another one started. His jaw grazed her temple. And his hot, tremulous whisper warmed her ear. "I can give you a baby, Laura."

A stillness overcame her. A heady, daunting stillness. "Wh-what?"

He shifted her in his arms and forced her to meet his serious, heart-stopping gaze. "I want to father your baby."

Her breath, it seemed, had left her. She felt stunned. Shaken. "Father my—" Panic flooded her then like an incoming tide. She was half in love with him now. What chance would she have of guarding her heart if they shared the miracle of childbirth? If they had a baby to bind them closer? "No, no, that...that won't work. I could never—"

"Shh." He touched a finger to her lips. Intensity simmered in his eyes. "Don't answer now." His dark face slanted across hers, then he kissed her with such sweet, lingering tenderness that her mind clouded, her blood warmed, and she could have wept. "Think about it," he urged. "Just think about it."

She couldn't help but do that very thing. She thought about it as he guided her off the dance floor, tossed money on their table, wrapped her coat around her and swept her to the door. She thought about it as he helped her into his car, and on the long, chilly drive home.

She could have a baby—*Cort's* baby.

When the force of her clashing emotions stoked too great a pressure inside her, she nearly gasped into the tense, leather-scented darkness of his car, "I don't understand why you're offering me this. You don't want a child."

"I do."

"You never did before!"

"I wasn't ready then. I am now."

"Why?"

He was silent for such a long while, she thought he had no answer. When he spoke, his voice emerged low and gruff. "Because I want someone of my own. Someone I can love. And who will love me." The heat of his gaze radiated through the winter darkness. "Always."

Emotion clogged her throat again. He was repeating her words, she knew, but he said them with such feeling she couldn't doubt he meant them.

She'd never heard him talk of love before. It made her heart clench with dangerous longing. "But I live in Memphis, and you're in Atlanta. How could we both share in our child's day-to-day life? I want him to be close to his father. To forge a tight bond. And even if you manage to do that from several states away, he'd always be saying goodbye to one of us. He'd always be missing one of us."

The silence ached and throbbed between them.

"A child would be damn lucky to have a mother who thinks like that, Laura. Who loves him enough to care about who he's missing." He shook his head in silent reflection. "How could I *not* want you as the mother of my children?"

And she felt herself falling, falling. Deeply. Hopelessly. Headlong...

"We don't have to live that far away from each other," he said. "We can figure something out."

It was true. She could move closer to him. Nothing tied her to Memphis. She could work just as well, if not better, in Altanta. And she could have his son, his daughter, who very well might have his hair, his eyes, his smile.

A son. Or daughter. Hers and Cort's.

A keen, painful, joyous yearning expanded her heart. And she knew, in that moment, that she had been fooling herself. She wouldn't have had Fletcher's baby, wouldn't have gone through with their parenting plan, no matter how he'd felt about her. Cort's reappearance in her life had canceled out that possibility.

Because she'd fallen in love with Cort, all those years ago, and again when she'd seen him at Steffie's, and at least a hundred times since. Deeper and deeper in love she fell, every time she was with him.

Why should she fool herself into believing otherwise?

He had offered to father her baby. She could allow herself that much of him...couldn't she? *Couldn't she?*

He guided the car into his driveway, between the towering oaks and magnolias, and parked in front of the house she already knew so well. The house she would tailor into "the place she most wanted to be."

She wouldn't be living here, though. Cort didn't love her, and she would never stand in his way of finding love, or torture herself by maintaining too close a daily contact. But her child could live here part of the time.

Her heart ached as much as it rejoiced.

Cort switched off the engine, climbed out of the car, strode around and opened her door. She took the hand he offered, strong, steady and somehow comforting. But his face...ah, his face. Taut, intense, determined.

Fear pulsed through her. She loved him too much. And loving Cort had once nearly destroyed her.

He swept her up the steps to his house with an iron-strong arm around her. Doubts skittered in her stomach. He unlocked the door, drew her inside and pushed the wool knit coat from her shoulders. It fell heedlessly to the floor of the entrance hall.

"Laura." He invoked her name like a gruff, earnest prayer, and held her shoulders between reverent hands. "Don't be afraid. I know what you want for your child. I want the same things."

She wished so much to believe that it could work. Strength and sureness emanated from him. And heat. And a heart-thrilling hunger...

"Come to bed with me," he implored in a torrid whisper, his gaze searing her. "Let's go upstairs, Laura. Let's make a baby."

She felt dizzy with longing. "We...we have to plan," she hedged. "Make arrangements."

"There's nothing to arrange. We don't need a damn clinic or some petri dish." He gripped her hips, and his thumbs swept in caressing arcs up and down her abdomen. "If a baby's going to grow inside you, I want to be the one to put it there."

Ardent heat flared in her. She wanted him. Wanted him! And she wanted his baby. Fear wouldn't stop her.

Cort saw the decision flash in her gaze; felt the change in chemistry. He'd seduced her into this moment, he knew. He'd used every inducement, pressed every advantage, to lure her here.

He'd won his chance. But only a chance.

Please, God, make it count.

Fierce need drummed like a driving beat in his temples, and his vision wavered with rays of heat. He thrust his arm around her back, caught her behind the knees and swept her up into his arms. She clung to him, her eyes dark with desire, her hair cascading over his arm, her maddening dress pushed high on her thighs.

He carried her to his room. To his bed.

And he worshiped her there. He feasted on her there. He stripped away her clothes, piece by piece, and filled his hands, his mouth with her. She writhed and arched and moaned and filled her hands, her mouth with him.

She goaded him into desperation.

Feverish with need, he pinned her beneath him, gritted his teeth and pushed deep, deep, into her. Fierce, hot pleasure took his breath. Stunned him. Electrified his blood.

He thrust harder. Slower. Slick, hot and deep. Rhythmic.

And she transformed, as he'd known she would, into a purely sensual being—striving to prolong each penetration with voluptuous undulations; shifting positions to maximize sensation; meeting him thrust for jarring thrust.

She riled him into savagery. Sweat dripped into his eyes. Groans rolled from his throat. He saw her through a passionate haze. *Beautiful. So damn beautiful.*

He forced her legs higher around his waist, levered his body for deeper access and drove with serious intent. He loved her. He needed her. He wanted his baby inside of her.

Her mouth opened. Her body moved with each deliberate, jolting thrust. And her dazed, heavy-lidded gaze sought his.

Pressure mounted within him. Her moans turned to sobs, then cries, and she jackknifed against his chest. Her velvet heat gripped him with tight contractions and plea-

sure pierced him, possessed him. He planted his seed deep
within her.

Please, God, make it count.

Please, God, make her mine.

10

FINGERS RIFFLED THROUGH her hair and brushed tendrils back from her face. A warm nuzzling against her neck made her squirm and smile. A smooth, strong jaw rubbed against her cheek. The pleasantly masculine scent of sandalwood aftershave teased her senses.

Laura opened her eyes.

Cort's dark, rugged face loomed above her. The warmth in his smiling blue eyes kindled an answering glow within her. "Morning," he greeted.

She smiled and ran her hand tenderly over the planes of his face. "Morning." And memories of their passionate, sumptuous night flooded back.

A remnant of the heat they'd shared warmed his eyes, and she wanted to feel his arms around her. She realized then that he was sitting on the bed, not lying in it, as she'd expected. And he was fully dressed, casually elegant in a light sage-colored shirt and charcoal-gray sport coat.

She, meanwhile, lay naked beneath the sheet.

"I have to meet with my real estate broker," he said in answer to her unspoken question. "Unavoidable, or I'd cancel. I might be tied up until three or so." He leaned in and brushed his mouth alongside her ear. "But I didn't want to leave without a kiss," he whispered.

"A kiss?" Her eyes rounded, and she caught his face between her hands to stave him off. She hadn't brushed her teeth yet! She couldn't possibly kiss him. "No. No kiss!"

"Now, Laura. After all we did last night, you can't be shy about something as tame as a kiss." She saw the mischievous glint in his eyes and knew he remembered darn well that she never kissed anyone in the morning before she brushed her teeth! Scoundrel that he was, he tilted his face and advanced.

With a protesting cry, she averted her mouth. He pinned her arms beside her head and dug his chin into her neck. She laughed and struggled. He kissed his way to her face, and she twisted beneath him to get away. An impromptu wrestling match ensued, as it often had in mornings at the Hays Street house, when the tussle usually degenerated into breathless laughter and the sweetest early-morning lovemaking.

But even then, she hadn't kissed him before brushing her teeth. A girl had to draw the line somewhere.

He soon had her shrieking in laughter from playful attacks and fending him off with shoulders, elbows and knees.

The phone rang. The answering machine clicked on, and a man spoke. Cort cursed, raised up and reached for the bedside phone. A business call. She took immediate advantage and scampered away, tugging the sheet off the bed and wrapping it around her as she dashed from his bedroom to her bathroom.

Moments after she'd locked the door, he said from directly outside the bathroom, "Okay. You win. Brush your teeth. But make it quick. I'm already late. And I'm not leaving without a kiss."

Laughter gurgled in her throat. She brushed her teeth, washed her face, combed her hair and slid into the white, terry-cloth robe she'd left on the hook. "You're a savage, Cort Dimitri," she called through the door.

"You bring it out in me, Laura Merritt. And you have

ten more seconds to open this door, or I'll use my master key."

"You have a master key?" She opened the door and poked her head out. "You're just so *masterful*."

He pounced. He pulled her out of the doorway, braced her against the bedroom wall and nipped at her mouth with light, smiling kisses, then delved more deeply.

The heat ignited in her again. She slid her fingers into his thick, raven hair and reveled in the hot, arousing taste of him. He groaned, then wrapped one hand around her nape and slid the other beneath her robe to roam freely.

The kiss deepened. The heat grew serious.

He forced himself to stop. Exhaling a long breath, he pressed his face to hers. "I'll be home as soon as I can," he rasped, his eyes closed, his body taut and hard, "and we'll pick up where we left off."

Her heart thundered. She didn't want to let him go. But of course, she did. His departing gaze left her weak-kneed and breathless.

She knew she should be worried. She was too emotionally involved. They'd made love all night—urgently, then tenderly. Teasingly. Insatiably.

How could he possibly make love to her like that if his emotions weren't engaged? *Don't be naive*, an inner voice warned. *Don't confuse sex with love...or history will repeat itself.* Yes, she should definitely worry.

But not today. Not when there was a chance that Cort's baby was growing inside her. She placed her hands wonderingly against her abdomen. She could be pregnant at this very moment!

With a rueful grin at her own irrepressible excitement, she hurried to take a shower. She had a lot of windows to measure before Cort returned. She also had ideas to sketch for the bedroom at the end of the hall, which she believed would make an adorable nursery.

A nursery. *For their baby*. Hers and Cort's.

Smiling to herself, she dressed in dark, slim-fitting jeans and a red sweater—red for Christmas, since today *was* the first of December. What a wonderful house to decorate for Christmas, she thought dreamily. She knew exactly where she'd put the tree. She hummed as she hooked dangling gold hoops into her ears.

The telephone rang, the answering machine clicked on, and a message piped through the intercom. "Cort, darling. Trisha. It's too, *too* bad of you to cry off from the duchess's party this Saturday, isn't it?" The feminine, throaty voice flowed with a rich British accent. "I had *such* a lovely idea for after the party. Give me a ring, won't you, and let me know when you'll be in London, you naughty boy." She didn't leave a number.

Laura sat down on the bed with an unpleasant rush of her heart. No reason to be upset, she told herself. He had, after all, "cried off" from the party. But he would be returning to London eventually. Maybe often.

Of course he had women. *Of course* he dated. She hadn't believed otherwise, had she?

The *duchess's* party. Was that someone's nickname, or did he schmooze with royalty while he jetted around the globe?

And what grounds did Trisha have for calling him a "naughty boy"?

Laura shut her eyes and forced herself to get a grip on her volatile emotions. Cort didn't owe her fidelity. She had known that before she'd slept with him. She had also known that he'd built a rich and varied life in which she played no part. Could she tolerate that fact, and possibly interact with the other women in his life, if she were raising a child with him?

A picture flashed across her mind's eye of her child jetting off to London with Cort for a romp around the castle grounds with Trisha.

Oh, my. An attitude adjustment was definitely needed. Or else, a drastic change in plans.

She'd be playing the role of ex-wife, she realized, without ever having had him as a husband. How could she bear to do that when she loved him? If she was already pregnant, she wouldn't have a choice!

Determined to put the anxiety aside until her emotions had settled and she could think clearly, she busied herself measuring windows.

A noise caught her attention—the sound of a door opening. The kitchen door. Laura wondered if Cort had come home early. Her heart beat faster at the thought.

What was she going to do? Sleep with him again, despite her reservations about having his baby? Tell him about those reservations, despite the abject humiliation of having to admit that she'd fallen in love with him again?

The murmur of a woman's voice mingled with a child's in the kitchen. Surprised and curious, Laura set down her measuring tape and ventured toward the sounds.

A stout, friendly-eyed woman with scraggly wisps of brown hair streaming from a haphazard topknot stood near the sink with a pitcher in her hand. "Oh, hello," she greeted in surprise at the sight of Laura. "I'm Judy Jeffries, the housekeeper. Hope I didn't startle you. I didn't know anyone was here."

"I hope I didn't startle *you.* I'm Laura Merritt. I'm a decorator, working here for a few days. Did I hear a child's voice, too?" She looked around the kitchen, but saw no child.

"My grandson, Duncan, just ran out to the car to get his coloring book. I bring him with me on Thursday mornings while my daughter works." Judy gave her a quick, curious once-over. "So...you're the new decorator, huh?"

Laura wondered at the odd way she'd phrased the question. Not *a* decorator, but *the new* decorator. "Um, yes."

A definite glint of curiosity lurked in Judy's gaze.

The door swung open and a small blond boy of about four or five traipsed into the kitchen holding a coloring book and crayons. "Grandma, I can't find the purple. Oh, hi." He regarded Laura with friendly, curious eyes, much like his grandmother's. Before he said another word, though, he looked beyond Laura and exclaimed, "Where's the table? I always color at the table. Where did it go?"

Laura glanced behind her at the empty kitchen, then back to the boy. He seemed to think that a table had been there. But Cort had told her that the only tables were in his bedroom. They'd had to eat breakfast on the courtyard-pavilion porch for that very reason.

"Duncan," said Judy, looking oddly flustered, "why don't you go outside and color? Duncan!" Judy bustled across the kitchen after him as he loped off toward the main rooms.

"Hey, *everything's* gone!" he yelled from the formal living room. His amazed tones echoed throughout the house. "Look, Grandma. The couches, the chairs...even the pictures are gone!" Judy lunged for his arm, but he evaded her, clutching his small box of crayons and coloring book as he ran. "The naked-lady statue is gone, too!" he shouted from the entrance hall.

"Uh, Duncan," Laura piped up, thoroughly puzzled. He really believed there had been furniture, pictures and naked-lady statues the last time he'd been here, which, according to what Judy had said, would have been last

Thursday. But Cort had clearly told her that the house hadn't had any furniture or artwork since he'd moved in. *Other than a couple bedrooms, it's as bare as a barn,* he'd said. "Are you sure you're thinking of the right house? I mean, your grandmother probably takes you with her to more than one house when she cleans, doesn't she?"

"Nope. Mr. D.'s the only one who lets me come. Tell her, Grandma," he appealed to Judy, troubled that his credibility was being questioned. "Didn't there used to be couches and pictures and stuff?"

One glance at Judy's hesitant face told Laura the truth. There *had* been. And Judy didn't want to tell her.

But that made no sense!

Judy bribed Duncan with a handful of cookies to go outside, then turned to Laura with a worried, apologetic gaze. "I hope this isn't going to cause problems. Mr. Dimitri asked me not to mention his moving all the furniture out of the house."

Laura gaped at her in stark disbelief. She couldn't believe he'd done such a thing, nor could she understand why. Was it furniture from the previous owner—something he didn't like? But even so, why had he lied to her about it?

"I believe he wants me to keep quiet about getting rid of everything so word doesn't get around about the other decorator. You know, he doesn't want to hurt her professional reputation."

"The *other* decorator?"

"The one who was here in August, when he bought all that stuff. She filled every room slap full."

"He had the house professionally decorated in August?"

Judy bit her lip, clearly realizing that she'd made matters worse. "I don't understand rich people, Ms. Merritt. They can be so eccentric."

LAURA SAT ON the edge of the bed in the guest room, her hand wrapped painfully tight around the telephone receiver. Cort would be home anytime now, and she desperately needed to understand the situation before she confronted him. She called the only person she knew who might have some insight. "I'm sorry if I pulled you away from a class, Steffie. It's not exactly an emergency, but I'm trying to make sense of things, and I really, really need your help."

"You didn't pull me away from class. I was at lunch," Steffie assured her, sounding concerned. "What's wrong?"

"Tell me, *please*—why did Cort hire me to decorate his house?"

The lengthy pause that followed only heightened Laura's tension. When Steffie finally answered, she sounded...cautious. "I assume because he wants his house professionally decorated."

"He had the house professionally decorated in August."

"He did? You're kidding!"

"And that's not the worst of it. After buying a household of furniture, he moved it all out last weekend, before I got here. He deliberately deceived me into thinking it's been empty since he bought it. He lied to me, Stef! I've never known him to do that. I feel that I don't really know him at all."

"Aw, Laur, no. Don't take this so hard. I know the thing with the furniture must seem like a lie, and in a way, I guess it is, but...but..." she lapsed into conflicted silence "...Cort had the very best intentions, I promise you."

"Best intentions?" The phrase doused her with foreboding. "What do you mean, 'best intentions'?"

Steffie hesitated, then burst out, "Oh, heck! This is all my fault. I should have listened to Tamika. She warned me that you'd end up hurt, and you are hurt, aren't you? I'm so sorry."

"What the hell are you talking about, Steffie?" Laura asked sharply, her alarm growing.

"You have to understand, Laura...Tamika, B.J. and I were worried sick over your plans to have a baby with Fletcher. I just heard this morning that you two called it off, and I can't tell you how relieved I am. Fletcher told B.J., and B.J. called Tamika, and Tamika—"

"I get the point. You've all been discussing my personal business as if I don't have enough sense to run my own life." Although she managed to keep her voice reasonably quiet, she couldn't help the anger that threaded through it.

"I understand why you might take it like that, but—"

"What does my plan with Fletcher have to do with Cort hiring me to decorate his house?" she interrupted, needing desperately to know.

Again, Steffie paused, then said in a deliberately low, calm voice that was obviously meant to soothe, "Cort was only doing what he thought was best. And so were we, because we all love you and care about you."

"Cut to the chase, Stef!"

"Please don't take this the wrong way, but when you said your appointment at the clinic was Wednesday, we had to find a way to stop you, at least long enough for you to think it over."

Laura felt the blood drain from her face in a nauseating *whoosh*. "You intentionally kept me from my clinic appointment? All of you? You discussed it, and planned it...and then Cort hired me to decorate his house as part of the scheme?" The shock of that revelation left her reeling.

"Well, it wasn't exactly like that. Cort came up with the

scheme on his own. Oh! No! I mean— He didn't come up with the *scheme*, but with the idea of hiring you."

"That's why he insisted I start right away," Laura stated with a sickening lurch of her heart. "To get me to break my appointment."

"To slow you down for a while. To give you time to reconsider. For your own good," Steffie stressed.

"Oh, please...!"

"Face the facts, Laura." Steffie's voice rose to match the volume and sharpness of Laura's. "The only reason you considered having a baby with a platonic friend is because you're afraid to get seriously involved with a man. You run from the first hint of intimacy. You can't blame us for worrying about what's going to happen to you, because you're not the kind of person who can live without love."

Laura's heart rose so high in her throat she couldn't respond. She wanted to lash out at Steffie—at all of them, including Cort. *Especially* Cort. But she couldn't argue with what Steffie had just said. She had run from relationships. She had preferred the safety of a platonic friendship.

And intimacy terrified her now more than ever.

But they still had no right to interfere in her life so intrusively. And Cort...! She couldn't bear to think about Cort.

"Maybe I feel more personally involved than I should," Steffie admitted in a choked voice that edged on tears, "because my brother was the one who hurt you so much. I'd do anything to help you get back to the person you were before he broke your heart. And I believe Cort would, too."

Laura sat in stunned silence. Could she be right?

"You mean, Cort feels guilty for hurting me..." Laura said, working her way through a painful jumble of thoughts "...and thinks that he's responsible for my...my avoidance of intimate relationships?"

"Well, isn't he?"

"No! I'm the one responsible for the choices I make. No one else. No one else has the right to claim responsibility."

The silence stretched between them like an unscalable wall.

"I'm sorry that I've upset you so much, Laura. Please believe that we all just wanted you to be happy. And I might be wrong about Cort's feelings, since he never talks about them. But whether he was acting out of guilt or just plain concern, I do know he invited you to decorate his house because he cares about you."

"Thank you for your honesty in telling me all this." Laura's voice was a strained whisper. "Having a baby with Fletcher would have been a terrible mistake, and I *am* glad I realized it before things went any further. I believe I would have canceled that clinic appointment on my own, but who knows? Maybe you did me a favor." *Unless I've already conceived Cort's baby.*

STEFFIE HAD CRIED A LITTLE, and told Laura again how much she loved her. By the time they hung up, they'd agreed to put the matter behind them.

Laura hoped that would be possible. She hoped no one would ever have to know about the *real* mistake she had made; the one with the potential to destroy the very fabric of her life.

What a fool she'd been, making love with Cort last night.

At least now, the puzzle pieces had fallen into place. She had no doubt that Cort had acted for "her own good." She believed that he did indeed care about her. She also knew he felt guilty for hurting her all those years ago. He'd apologized for it at Steffie's. He'd talked to her about her fear of intimate relationships, and tried to make her see that she was making a mistake with Fletcher. In return, she had cursed at him and swore that she hated him for hurting her, using her, scorning her.

Why shouldn't he believe that he'd traumatized her in a lasting way? And if he believed that, he would certainly feel guilty. He was now clearly trying to make amends... *even if he had to father her baby himself.*

An anguished cry tore from her. She shut her eyes and gripped the nightstand for balance.

She should have seen the truth for herself. He'd asked her why she wanted a baby so badly. She'd literally cried on his shoulder trying to explain. And while she had, he must have felt responsible—not only for hurting her fifteen years ago, but for his part in breaking up her plan with Fletcher; ruining her chance at motherhood.

And he should feel guilty for that! He'd had no right to interfere. Although her breakup with Fletcher had not been Cort's fault—and she did not regret it—she couldn't overlook the fact that Cort had plotted and lied. Even worse, he may have taken her to bed for reasons she hadn't understood.

Guilt could be a powerfully motivating factor...but not one she wanted involved in his decision to father her baby.

And guilt was certainly not what she'd been hoping he felt toward her. Despite all the lessons she'd learned from him, despite her firm resolve to avoid making the same mistake twice, she had begun to hope, in her heart of hearts, that Cort might be falling in love with her.

The pain of disillusionment hit her with a more crushing force than it had fifteen years ago.

And this time, she could be carrying his baby.

BUSINESS HAD KEPT HIM a little longer than he'd expected. It had seemed like an eternity. He'd had a hell of a time concentrating on offers, counteroffers and contractual details when thoughts of Laura kept drifting through his mind. He left the negotiating table the moment the deal had been closed and headed home.

Home. To Laura. Knowing she'd be there filled him with a heady warmth. Thinking about her laughter this morning made him smile. He wondered if she'd been thinking about him. He wondered if she was pregnant with his baby.

He wanted that so damn much. He wanted to be the daddy in her child's life. *His* child's life. He wanted to be the man at their breakfast table. The one who came home to them, and helped fight their battles, and took part in all their plans. He wanted to make love to her and only her for the rest of his life. He wanted her to be desperately in love with him.

It could all start with a baby.

He made an impulsive detour on his way home to a grocery store where he bought ice cream and pickles. He would ask her if she'd been craving either, or both. She would laugh, and say he was getting way ahead of himself. He would kiss her until the laughter and the teasing turned into passion. And then he'd take her to his bed.

Feeling vitally alive, he parked the car in the garage and strode into the house through the kitchen door, the small grocery sack tucked under his arm. "Laura?" he called, glancing casually into rooms as he passed by them. His call echoed through the house. Funny, but even with the echo and the lack of furnishings, the house no longer felt empty. "Laura?"

She didn't answer, and he headed toward the main stairway, wondering where and how he'd find her. In his bedroom, maybe...ready to pick up where they'd left off?

Before he reached the stairway, though, he came to a

dead halt. The most unexpected sight met his eyes. Her luggage. Stacked near the front door. He stared at it in puzzlement. And then foreboding. Dread.

She appeared, then, not from the top of the stairs as he'd expected, but from the drawing room. He knew the moment his gaze locked with hers that something had changed between them. The tender warmth and the alluring glow had given way to cool reserve. She'd reverted to the woman she had been at Steffie's last week. Distant. Wary. Untouchable.

Everything in him rebelled. She couldn't do that! She couldn't shove aside all that they had together. Couldn't take away what he needed so badly. Why would she want to leave him? Had she realized he'd fallen in love with her? Was she running, as everyone had warned him she would? Was she cutting him out of her life, as she had Fletcher?

She broke the silence between them with a quiet, simple statement. "You had your house professionally decorated in August."

He struggled to understand. She was withdrawing from him, leaving him... because of *the house*? It made no sense. The house meant nothing! Even his deception regarding the house meant nothing. At least, not enough to end their relationship. And he had no doubt that she intended to do just that. Dazed and reeling from the blow, he murmured, "July. It was July."

She tilted her head and studied him in cool detachment. "You stripped the place bare before I came."

"I wanted you here," he whispered.

"Why?"

How the hell to answer? From the moment he'd seen her at Steffie's, he'd wanted her back in his arms, his bed, his life. But he couldn't risk saying that now. Not when her bags sat near the front door and her gaze remained profoundly impersonal. He'd seen how she dealt with men who wanted more than she could give. "I thought I made that clear," he said. "I want you to make this house a home. I want *your* touch here, not someone else's. Your warmth. Your magic."

"You want my professional services," she translated, as if clearing up any possible misconception his words might create. "So you felt justified in...withholding the truth?"

He felt a flush rise beneath his skin. He had hated lying to her. And he hated defending the lie, even though his defense was God's honest truth. "I didn't think you'd come if you knew I'd had the place decorated. You'd already hesitated to accept my investment offer, and questioned my motives for making it. Besides if you *had* accepted the job knowing that I'd recently bought almost everything in the house, you wouldn't have felt free to disregard it all and start over. I took that obstacle out of our path."

She stared at him and the silence somehow became personal. "Did you conspire with Steffie, Tamika and B.J. to keep me from my clinic appointment?"

Utter dismay washed through him. She'd obviously talked to one of them. He knew he should have forced Steffie and her cohorts out of his room before they'd embroiled him in their discussion. They probably did believe that he'd conspired with them. But he hadn't. His investment offer and everything that followed had come straight from his own devious mind...and heart. He'd intended to keep Laura from that clinic appointment the moment he'd learned of it. No one else's input had affected him in the least. "I've never 'conspired' with anybody."

"Are you saying that you were not trying to stop me from pursuing my plans with Fletcher?"

He swallowed a frustrated curse. He wouldn't lie to her

again, ever. But he couldn't tell her the truth. He couldn't tell her he loved her, that the prospect of her having a baby and raising a child with another man nearly tore him apart. He had to act with caution, extreme caution, if he didn't want to lose all chance of forging a permanent bond with her. Of sharing a lifetime of intimate moments. Of finding a back door to her heart.

"I felt you were making a serious mistake," he admitted cautiously. "And you weren't listening to anything I had to say about the matter."

"Do you know why?" Her eyes flashed, and she didn't wait for an answer. "Because my personal plans with Fletcher were *none of your business.*"

Ridiculous, how much that hurt. "Let's go sit down and talk about this." He turned toward the kitchen, away from her gaze, with his sack of ice cream and pickles still tucked under his arm. She damn sure wouldn't laugh now, if he gave them to her.

"You're not headed for the kitchen, are you?" she called from behind him. At least she was following him. "There's no table or chairs in here," she pointed out when they arrived. "Or did you forget? The only table or chairs are *in your bedroom.*"

He resisted the urge to wince. How devious must *that* seem to her? He shoved the ice cream into the freezer, set the pickles aside and turned to face her. Anger glistened in her eyes. He'd never been gladder to see it there. Her impersonal coldness had been cutting him to the quick.

"So then let's go to my bedroom," he quietly replied, his gaze probing hers.

Vulnerability flashed across her face.

His love for her leaped and glowed. "What difference does it make where we are? We can sit and talk in my bedroom just as easily as we can make love here on the kitchen floor."

She backed away with something like alarm. "I shouldn't have come here."

He shifted closer, needing to take her in his arms. "Laura—"

She held up a halting hand. "No, don't." She took a moment for some internal struggle, then reclaimed her poise. The distancing coolness had returned. "Your honesty meant a lot to me, Cort. I believed I could trust anything you said. And that trust was one of the most important reasons I thought I could raise a child with you."

Alarm coursed through him. He took hold of her shoulders, urgently seeking an emotional connection. "We *can* raise a child together," he swore. "We *will*."

"I hope that won't be necessary."

Those softly whispered words jolted him. *She no longer wanted his baby.* He probably should have deduced as much, but he hadn't. The sense of loss and rejection staggered him.

He'd brought it on himself, he knew. He couldn't deny that. He *had* lied. He *had* schemed. And now he wanted more than ever to explain why. But wasn't this exactly how Fletcher had met his fate, wanting her too much to hold back the damning words?

"I...I care about you, Laura." *Pitifully inadequate.* "I never meant to hurt you. That's...that's the exact opposite of what I meant to do."

Her expression changed in the most baffling way. As if he'd somehow hurt her again. But the anger and emotional distance had vanished. Her voice, when she spoke, sounded sad and wistful. "I know you care about me, Cort." The smile she gave him was fraught with troubled affection and regret. "I realize your intentions were good.

And your offer to father my baby was..." she paused and swallowed "...touching."

"Touching?" He didn't like the sound of that.

"And maybe I owe you my thanks, in a way."

Her thanks. *Oh, God...* "In what way?"

"Your presence did force Fletcher's feelings for me out into the open, which helped settle things in my mind. At least now I know the truth about him."

The truth about him. As if he'd committed some unforgivable crime.

"But more important than that," she continued, "I've learned something about myself in the past few days. I've realized that platonic friendship isn't enough. And neither is a purely sexual relationship."

Purely sexual. She had to be talking about him. Did she still see their relationship in that light?

"Maybe I have been running from intimacy, as everyone seems to think." She drew in a breath, glanced at the ceiling with eyes that grew too shiny, then forced her gaze back to his. "But I'm over that now. I realize what I need. A relationship that has it all—friendship, passion and *love.* You understand that, don't you? I want to...to fall in love. With someone who will love me. And I hope, I pray, that a baby will come from that union, and no other."

He stared at her, his throat locked up with the most incredible pain. Moments ago, she'd made it clear that she no longer wanted his baby. And now she'd explained why. A "purely sexual" relationship wasn't enough. She wanted to fall in love.

In her infinitely gentle way, she'd said to him exactly what he'd said to her fifteen years ago. That all they had between them was sex. And that she didn't love him.

Or had he misunderstood? As unlikely as that seemed, he had to be sure, absolutely sure. He couldn't let her drift out of his life if there was any chance that she might yet fall in love with him. But he couldn't jeopardize their future relationship with full honesty in case she was, in fact, carrying his child. His raspy whisper scalded his raw throat. "Do you have any particular man in mind?"

Deep, complex emotion roiled in her gaze. The most obvious was reluctance to answer. "No," she finally whispered. "But I'm sure I'll find him some day."

And he suddenly understood why she, in her compassion, broke contact with men who showed signs of serious attachment—to avoid ripping out their very hearts and souls.

11

IT WOULD TAKE about two weeks from the night they'd made love, Laura estimated, before she would know if she was pregnant. She had promised Cort she'd call him the moment she knew.

Two weeks!

She'd barely made it through that first day back in Memphis. How would she ever make it through the intervening days? The uncertainty was torture. The pain of living without Cort was worse. She couldn't stop thinking about him. Craving his company, his smile, his touch. Loving him.

She tried to comfort herself with the knowledge that she had done the honorable thing. She had relieved his mind, she hoped, of the idea that he'd traumatized her into a fear of intimate relationships. She had convinced him that she was ready to find love.

But that was one thing she would never do. Because the man she loved—the only man she would *ever* love—did not love her. That much was obvious. He hadn't tried to stop her from leaving. He'd driven her to the airport with barely a word; hugged her, and watched her board the plane. He'd broken her heart again, and didn't even know it.

She'd done the right thing, cutting their ties.

But those ties couldn't be completely cut if she turned out to be pregnant. Her emotions at this possibility swung like a pendulum from moment to moment. She fervently prayed she wasn't, then desperately hoped she was. She knew she should stay far, far away from Cort Dimitri and the heartbreak he would always bring her...yet she wanted more than anything to have his baby. *Their baby.*

The only relief she found during the first few days away from Cort was through her work. She buried herself in projects, including the design of his house. She also spent time with Fletcher, choosing furniture, artwork and other antiques for Cort.

Though she felt somewhat of a strain with Fletcher at first, they soon fell back into a semblance of the roles they'd established over fifteen years. He'd mentioned that Cort was investing two hundred thousand in his business. Laura was glad for him.

Fletcher also talked about B.J. quite a bit. She'd spent the week with him, photographing antiques to sell over the Internet. Laura suspected that her presence at that particular time had to do with the conspiracy to sabotage their parenting plan, but she refrained from pointing this out. It seemed that B.J. planned to travel with him to an upcoming auction. Laura was pleased Fletcher had found company.

She, on the other hand, spared no time for socializing, not even for Christmas activities. Her project of designing the interior of Cort's house absorbed her for hours every day. Although her assistant had agreed to handle all personal contact with him—a request that had raised eyebrows—Laura prepared samples, sketches, photos and a disk of layouts to ship to him.

She wondered what he'd think of her "vision." He'd been adamant about giving her free rein, but she worried he might be disappointed. She couldn't allow herself to dwell on that, though. She'd already wasted too much time thinking about him, missing him, wondering where he was and whom he was with. Trisha, maybe, in London? Some other woman, who now played, laughed and loved with him in the very rooms she was designing?

Her heart ached. The days crawled by.

Steffie and Tamika both called her during that first week, concerned that she might be feeling down because of her foiled plan for motherhood. Laura tried her best to persuade them she was fine. She forced a cheerful demeanor, but the effort drained her.

She told no one, *no one*, about the possibility that she carried Cort's baby. He had agreed to keep the matter confidential. There'd be time enough to break the news to friends if and when she knew for certain she was pregnant. That possibility hovered in her mind relentlessly throughout the first week.

One more excruciating week to go before her period was due.

She prayed that she wasn't pregnant. She prayed that she was.

CORT SPENT OVER a week on the road, tending to business in New York and London. He tried to engross himself with an aggressive new project as well as those already on the table.

But at night, alone in hotel suites, he thought of nothing but Laura. He missed her with an ache that wouldn't quit. Things she'd said, things they'd done, played ceaselessly in his head. Worse, though, were the dreams when he'd wake to the scent of her; the taste of her. The heat of her kiss.

She wanted to fall in love. And he, as always, was the wrong man.

What the hell would he do if she was carrying his baby? Just hearing her talk about finding her true love some day pierced him with intolerable pain. He couldn't imagine how he'd survive raising a child with her while she made a life with another man.

But what the hell would he do if she *wasn't* carrying his baby? He would have no ties with her. No contact. No shared moments. That seemed worse, much worse, than anything he could imagine.

He returned home on a Monday afternoon, twelve days after she'd left him. Only a few more days, he assumed, before he would know if their lives would intertwine.

The Yuletide music on the radio and the Christmas lights blazing on houses he passed provoked more memories, but from the distant past. Fifteen years had gone by since he'd spent a Christmas with her, but this time of year always reminded him of Laura. *Any* holiday reminded him of Laura.

In December, she'd have Christmas lights burning, friends stringing popcorn to wrap around the tree—whether they wanted to or not—and a wonderland of holly, bows and elves. At Halloween, she'd have pumpkins and whatnot. Hell, she even decorated for Arbor Day with little trees. He couldn't look at a holiday decoration without thinking of Laura.

And now the sight of his house reminded him of her, too. He motored up the drive and the mansion loomed before him, dark and vacant. Deserted. The ache in his gut began to throb. She'd been starry-eyed and passionate over this place. She would have had lights, and wreaths, and candles in every window.

He unlocked the door, walked in, switched on the entrance-hall light. The massive emptiness of the house bore down on him. A shell of a house, it seemed. And no amount of expensive items or furnishings would ever make a difference. He saw no beauty in its architectural details; gleaned no pleasure from its history, or satisfaction from its worth. He couldn't recapture the sense of home.

He'd never think of it as anything other than "the place he most wanted her to be."

He would have to keep busy to make it through this night. And the next week. *The rest of his life...*

He damn sure couldn't distract himself with a swim. Going anywhere near the pool would be masochistic. He could hardly bear standing here in the entrance hall, where he'd swept her into his arms and carried her up to his bed. He had no desire to gravitate toward the kitchen where that silly gallon of ice cream and jar of pickles would mock him. He couldn't think of a single room that wouldn't smother him with memories.

He settled for leafing through his mail. He let out an ironic laugh at the sight of a neatly addressed package. The return address read, *Laura Merritt Design Associates*. There was no escaping her. He took the package to the only room with chairs—his bedroom. *His bedroom*, for God's sake. Sensory images of their lovemaking nearly forced him out of the door.

He had to face up to her absence, though. Weather the worst of the storm. Hadn't he survived this same trauma when he'd left her fifteen years ago? Hadn't he eventually learned how to breathe again, how to function again, without dying a little each moment?

Only by burying the purest, finest part of himself for fifteen years.

He avoided his bed and sat in an armchair to open the package she'd sent him. Not too surprisingly, he found her plans for the house. Sketches, samples, photos and a computer disk. He wasn't in the mood to look at anything to do with the house, but he hungered for communication with her; for any kind of connection.

He slowly perused each photo and sketch, then inserted the disk into his laptop computer. Illustrations lit the screen of how each finished room would look.

A sense of awe overtook him. She'd done exactly as he'd hoped. Even gazing at the scenes on a computer screen didn't stop the magic from happening. Rooms he'd never spent much time in beckoned with new appeal. Corners he'd barely noticed suddenly caught his eye. Colors soothed. Intrigued. Provoked a whimsical longing...

But then specific details drew his attention and evoked a very different response. A particular Oriental carpet...a wide, wing-backed chair...an antique armoire...a unique style of draperies...artwork from his favorite masters.

A prickling sensation crept up the back of his neck. He hadn't made any of these selections for Laura. Yet here they were, the very things he'd personally chosen last July for the other decorator—the *only* things he'd personally chosen out of the household of furnishings he'd ended up buying. He had these items, or ones strikingly similar, stored carefully in a warehouse.

How had Laura known so specifically what would appeal to him? How had she woven these things so seamlessly with her own ideas, creating a mood and theme all her own? Everywhere he looked in these renderings, he saw her. And him. Together.

He pulled the disk out of the computer and shoved it along with the photos and samples into a dresser drawer. He couldn't think about the house right now, or her vision for it, or how damn much he wanted her here. She wasn't his. She never would be. He had to find a way to live despite those facts.

The phone rang. He answered it, ill-tempered but grateful for any distraction.

"Cort? Fletcher. Had a question about the contract you sent me."

Cort listened to the question, which proved to be an intelligent, straightforward one. He answered without hesitation. He'd been impressed with the proposal Fletcher had submitted and with his professionalism throughout their discussions. Cort knew that maintaining the businesslike demeanor couldn't be easy for him, considering Fletcher believed that Laura was in love with Cort.

Another shaft of pain sliced through him. Fletcher had been wrong about that.

"Uh, by the way, Cort." Fletcher cleared his throat. "About Laura."

He tensed at the mention of her name. He hadn't expected Fletcher to bring up the subject, an understandably delicate one between them. They'd both wanted her. And she had shut them both out of her heart. He clutched the phone harder. "What about her?"

"Has she talked to you lately?"

Cort frowned. Was he rubbing in the fact that she'd left him? No. The guy cared more about the two-hundred-thousand-dollar investment he was about to make than that. "What do you mean, 'talked to me'? About what?"

"Anything. The way she's feeling, I guess. I know she talks to Steffie and Tamika...or at least, she used to. She used to open up to me, too, but that was before, uh...well, you know." He hesitated, and Cort wanted to reach through the phone line and shake the words out of the guy. "There might not be anything to worry about."

"But you think there is?" Cort prompted, his impatience and concern growing.

"Hell, I don't know," Fletcher muttered. "She looks okay. She's been acting her usual cheerful self, and she's got Tamika and Steffie convinced she's fine. But..."

"But what?" Cort bit out, the very softness of his voice a threat.

"She hasn't put up any Christmas decorations."

Cort held the phone in stunned silence.

"B.J. went to her house with some photos of furniture and noticed she didn't have a tree. It's already December twelfth. Laura usually has a tree up on the first. Anyway, B.J. and I took a tree to her house...and she didn't put the first ornament on it. Not even those strings of popcorn."

Cort frowned. Squinted. Struggled to make some kind of sense out of it. *Not even the popcorn?*

"Well," Fletcher concluded, sounding somewhat embarrassed, "just thought maybe you should know."

"Yeah," Cort agreed, pondering the enigma with escalating concern. "Thanks."

Something had to be wrong. Drastically wrong. Was she depressed? If so, why? Was she ill? If so, with what? Was she simply too busy? No. If Laura were the leader of the free world, she'd find time to string popcorn around her Christmas tree.

Cort's heart tripped. His breath caught.

Was she...*pregnant?*

SNOW HAD BEGUN to fall in Memphis early that Tuesday morning, lightly dusting the parking lot surrounding her interior-design shop. Laura stared out the side window near her desk at the hypnotic swirl of lacy flakes.

She was functioning in a state of shock. Every beat of her heart echoed the news: pregnant. Pregnant! The circle had turned red on her test kit, less than an hour ago. Not just an iffy pink, but a sure, vibrant red. And though she'd tried to prepare herself for that possibility, she felt dazed and awed and overwhelmed. She hadn't told anyone yet. She barely believed it herself.

She had a baby growing inside of her! Cort's baby. *Her* baby. Sweet, keen joy coursed through her, followed closely by an ache. A familiar ache—the gnawing at her heart that had only grown worse every day since she'd left Cort.

She would have to call him, as soon as she had the positive result confirmed by a doctor. How would he take the news? Would he be happy, or disappointed? He'd come so close to being free of her. Would he see it that way? He'd said he wanted a baby. He'd deliberately set out to make her pregnant. But he'd done it as a favor to her, out of a sense of guilt and responsibility. She didn't want that from him. She didn't want that for her baby.

She closed her eyes with a sudden surge of yearning. If only he loved her!

Struggling to master her emotions, she forced her attention back to her work and copied catalog numbers onto an order form. Miriam, the posh yet motherly designer who had worked with Laura for years, advised a customer about upholstery selections. Janet, a quiet, shy young woman with the soul of a true artiste, sketched intently at the worktable.

"Laura," called Miriam from the front of the shop, "someone's here to see you."

Surprised, because most of her customers contacted her by phone and friends rarely dropped by the shop, Laura glanced up from her work.

Her heart flipped over and landed with a thud.

Cort.

She stared in shaken disbelief. She felt as if her secret news and tortured yearning had somehow joined forces to conjure him from thin air. Tall and broad-shouldered, his jet hair glinting with snowflakes, he stood with his hands in the pockets of a long, black cashmere overcoat. The crisp, white collar of a dress shirt contrasted with the swarthy bronze of his strong throat and jaw. His vivid blue-eyed gaze locked with hers.

Her pulse clamored. What was he doing here? Why had he come?

She rose slowly from behind her desk. She couldn't utter a single word of greeting. *He's the father of my baby.* Would she be forced to give him the news in person? She wasn't sure she could handle that. What emotion would she see in his eyes, if any?

She turned away from his potent gaze, her face warm, her pulse pounding. "Miriam, this is Cort Dimitri from Atlanta. You'll probably recognize his name from the file I gave you. Cort, Miriam Brenner. And this is Janet Ingram," she belatedly added as Janet gaped at Cort from another desk, looking dazed and smitten.

He murmured a greeting to both women, a groove deepening beside his mouth, although he had yet to smile. Laura was grateful that he hadn't. Her knees were weak enough as it was.

"Mr. Dimitri," Miriam welcomed with a suave smile, "how nice to meet you." She offered her hand and he took it. An intrinsically feminine glow lit her gently lined face. "I've fallen in *love* with your house from the photos. I'll be overseeing the project from this point on, so I'm the one to answer any questions you might have."

Laura had almost forgotten her instructions for Miriam to handle all correspondence with him. Maybe she could keep him occupied while Laura slipped out...and never came back....

"I'll keep that in mind, Miriam." His low, smooth voice reached inside Laura like a caress. "But I'm not here about the house. I've come to see Ms. Merritt." His gaze meandered from Miriam to her. "It's personal."

Warmth rushed to her head, making her feel slightly disoriented. A subtle vitality pulsed in the room. His virile presence electrified the very air she breathed.

Laura dreaded being alone with him. She'd longed for him too much. She wanted to feel his arms around her, his mouth on her. He didn't love her, and the heartbreak was so hard to live with. And now they'd have a child to raise. "I'm afraid I'm too busy to leave the shop. Maybe we can meet later." Her pulse raced. She needed time to collect herself...fortify her defenses....

"Come with me, Laura." It was a soft, gruff request. A command.

She longed to go. And feared the same.

"I'll mind the store," Janet piped up in her shy, quiet way. "You just go ahead."

"Go," urged Miriam. "Be sure to bundle up, hon." Before Laura could invent a plausible reason not to go, Miriam had helped her into her coat as Janet looped the strap of her purse over her arm.

And Cort watched her, *only* her, with a smoky intensity she knew only too well.

As if in a dream, she moved toward him. He opened the door for her and ushered her out with a light pressure at the small of her back, barely a touch, but she felt the heat of his hand through the thick wool of her coat. And then they were outside, walking toward a gleaming silver Mercedes sedan.

The bracing winter air rushed against her heated face and lifted tendrils of her hair, but she still felt overly warm. *Tell him. Tell him.* She couldn't! She had to get the pregnancy confirmed by a doctor first, she rationalized. *The circle was red, not pink,* her conscience argued. There was no doubt about the positive result.

But she was so afraid of what she would see or *not* see in his gaze. "Why are you here, Cort?"

He stopped beside the car, his expression brooding. "You turned my *file* over to someone else? Why? To avoid me?"

"No! I just...well..." she couldn't escape his probing gaze "...yes."

A muscle moved in his jaw. "Don't do that, Laura. Don't ever do that."

Her heart thudded. She had to force the conversation into safer channels. "Have you looked at my plans for your house?"

"Yes."

"Did you...?"

"Let's go somewhere private to talk. Your house. Where is it?"

She hesitated only a moment. She couldn't deny him the chance to speak with her alone. He was the father of her baby; he had rights. Inalienable rights. Like, the right to *know* he was the father of her baby! And they had many serious issues to discuss. Like...custody arrangements. Her heart contracted painfully. "My house is right there." She nodded toward the quaint side street with snowy sidewalks, small lawns, tall bare oak trees and old-fashioned houses with covered front porches. "The second house on the right."

He held out his hand to her. She hesitated to take it. She wanted to touch him in the worst way. But then she'd have to let him go. A frown gathered again in his eyes, and she reluctantly slipped her hand into his. He wove his long, dark fingers through hers, his palm hard and warm against her own, and pulled her deliberately close to him. Her heart pounded in her throat as they walked through the light dusting of snow to her house.

She'd been so lost. His touch, his nearness, his strength felt like a safe, warm harbor, if only a temporary one.

He halted on the walkway that led to her porch and peered at her house. She glanced at him, wondering why he was looking. She saw nothing out of the ordinary about the small, white, red-roofed bungalow.

"This is the right house," she assured him, thinking that maybe he doubted it.

He slanted her an unreadable glance. She climbed the porch steps and unlocked the door. He followed her inside and surveyed the small, neat living room with a bewildering frown. His gaze then lighted on the unadorned fir tree in the corner. "I wouldn't have believed it," he murmured, "if I hadn't seen it for myself." He turned his gaze to her. "Why haven't you decorated for Christmas?"

She blinked, taken aback. She'd never known Cort Dimitri to acknowledge the existence of holiday decorations, let alone look for them. "I...I haven't had time. I've been busy."

"Busy?" He unbuttoned his long, heavy cashmere coat and draped it over an armchair. "I know you better than that." He then unfastened the buttons of her coat. "I don't care how busy you were. By now you should have transformed this entire city block into the North Pole. What happened?"

She averted her face, unable to move away because of his hold on her coat. Incredible how his questions over a relatively frivolous concern provoked the urge to smile and to cry at the very same time. "I guess I haven't been in the mood."

He slipped the coat off of her, tossed it onto the chair and tipped her face up to his. "What mood have you been in?"

Dangerous, to expose herself this way to his probing

gaze. "Stressed," she whispered. "Because of the...uncertainty of...of everything." The truth. Unarguably the truth. But not all of it. Not by a long shot.

"You never handled stress this way before. If anything, it used to send you into a decorating frenzy." The mild humor in his tone contrasted with the intensity of his stare. "Have you been feeling...down?"

She bit her bottom lip to suppress a ridiculous quiver. She didn't have to answer him, but his concern and compassion were wearing down her already weakened defenses. "A little, maybe. Nothing to worry about, though." *I've missed you! Nothing seems important without you.* And she realized that a great deal of her fear had to do with that. How could she make her baby a happy home when she anguished so deeply over Cort? Would that ever change?

"I brought you something." He reached down for his coat, slid his hand into one of the pockets and brought out a flat, slim, red package wrapped in cellophane.

She stared at it as he placed the item in her hands. A lump swelled in her throat. "Microwave popcorn." Her vision wavered, and she choked back unshed tears, overcome by a sudden urge to hurtle herself into his arms. She sat blindly down onto the sofa. "To string around my tree."

He sat down beside her. "If you want to pop it, I'll, uh, you know...help string it."

And that, silly though it was, undid her. He was offering to string her popcorn! He *hated* to string popcorn. She'd had to badger him into it at the Hays Street house. A sob rose in her throat and she made a move to launch from the sofa.

He caught her by the shoulders. "Laura?" His dark face swam before her in patent concern.

Hot tears welled in her eyes. She buried her face in her hands and gave in to them.

He pulled her firmly into his embrace, running his hand up and down her back, sending tingling trails of heat through the silk of her blouse. "What's wrong?" he whispered against her hair. "Why are you crying? It's not something like that silly scarf again, is it?"

That made her laugh...which only made her cry harder. Why was she so emotional with him? Sure, she loved him. Sure, she couldn't have him, and he'd break her heart for the rest of her life, and she'd have to play the role of his ex-wife, but was that any reason to cry?

"I'm sorry," she croaked, pulling herself together with an effort and glancing at him apologetically. "I...I just haven't been feeling too well lately. And I'm t-tired. And I did try to string the popcorn last night, but I burned it. And the smell—" She shuddered, and her hand went to her stomach. "I just can't make popcorn right now. I don't mean to sound ungrateful, but—" The look in his eyes stopped her.

A troubling new intensity beamed from those midnight-blue depths—*not* the same kind of intensity she'd come to know. What did it mean?

She drew back nervously from his arms, found a tissue in her slacks pocket—she'd been needing them quite frequently lately—and dried her face. "We...we can string lights on the tree, if you'd like."

"You're pregnant," he breathed.

Not a question. Not a suggested theory. A statement.

If that wasn't just like him! She struggled to hold back tears again.

He grasped her face between his hands, and his gaze blazed a serious question—a demand for confirmation. "I'm not telling you anything you don't know. Am I?"

Her heart stood still. She prayed to see joy. *And love, please God.* Was that asking too much? "No," she whispered. "You're not telling me anything I don't know. The circle on my test kit turned red this morning."

Cort couldn't stop himself from staring at her. *Pregnant. With his baby.* A sense of awe swelled to such immensity within him that he could barely breathe. *His baby!* He would be a father. And she, the woman he loved, the woman he would always love, was the mother of his child. Nothing had prepared him for the visceral shock of this moment. Crazy, he knew, since he'd suspected the truth before he'd even left Atlanta. And when he'd seen her, that suspicion had only deepened. Something in her gaze and manner had alerted him to a profound change in her.

Something about that change troubled him.

Anguish, he realized, putting a name to it with a sickening thud of his heart. He sensed a low-key but very real anguish in her. Did she not want this baby? He remembered then that she'd whispered something to that effect just before she'd left him. She wanted a baby from the man she would eventually fall in love with...not from him.

And now he saw unbearable sadness in her, and he thought that he might die.

"Cort, I'm so sorry it turned out this way."

No. He didn't believe it. The Laura he knew would not be sorry. She couldn't possibly not want or love a baby she carried...and she would certainly cherish his. He had no doubt about that, just as he'd known that something was drastically wrong for her not to decorate for Christmas. *He knew her.* He might not know everything about her, having been apart for fifteen long years, but he knew the heart and soul and infinitely loving core of her.

Why, then, did anguish loom in her eyes?

"I was hoping so much," she whispered, "that you'd be happy."

For the second time in moments, he sat immobilized with shock. "Me? You hoped *I'd* be happy?"

"You don't have to make it sound so unlikely." A martial light ignited in the midst of her anguish, and Cort grappled with the realization that she thought he didn't want this baby. "I know you offered to father my child as a...a favor to me...."

"A favor?"

"...because you feel guilty for hurting me and responsible for my so-called 'fear of intimacy,' and maybe for breaking up my plan with Fletcher. But this baby—this precious, beautiful baby that we've made together—"

"Laura!" He caught her face between his hands, swept his thumbs across her tear-dampened skin, gazed at her with all the love that burned for her in his heart. "You *can't* believe that I don't want this baby. *Our* baby. I've prayed that you'd conceive. I prayed for it, Laura...even while we were making love."

She stared at him with astonishment, and his heart ached to think she hadn't known.

"Maybe I did feel guilty for hurting you," he said, "and responsible for the damage I'd done. But you don't know the worst of it."

"The worst?" she repeated. And he sensed she was bracing herself.

He, too, braced himself—for the possibility that the heartrending emotion he read in her face had to do with the baby and not with him at all. "I don't know how you feel about me, or if what I'm about to say will make you shut me out of your life. But I *have* been lying to you, Laura. Not only about the furniture in my house, or my reason for wanting you there. I've lied from the very first day I met you. I lied every time I kissed you, every time we made love. Because I let you think it was sex—only sex—when it never was to me." He scoured her face, her eyes, in a desperate search for tenderness, praying harder than he ever had. "I just love you so damn much."

A great, hot surge of joy rose in Laura, and her feelings for him radiated like a power source. How could he not have known that she loved him? How could he believe she would shut him out of her life for loving her? Too overcome to speak, she answered him with a kiss—a deep, joyous, needful kiss. Ah, yes, *needful*. She needed him as a vital, integral part of her heart and soul.

But the kiss wasn't enough, she knew. She had to tell him; to leave no doubt. Drawing back, she smiled lovingly into his eyes, and saw pain-filled questions still lurking there. "In case you're wondering, I *did* find my true love," she whispered. "At the Hays Street house. He owned the place, you see. I gave him my heart along with first month's rent. And he never gave it back. So I've been avoiding intimacy with other men because they're all the wrong men. He'll always be the only *right* man for me."

The finest, warmest happiness blazed in his gaze, burning away all doubt. Thrusting his fingers into her hair, he tipped her back against the sofa and kissed her with poignant, eloquent longing. "Marry me, Laura," he implored in a devout whisper. He kissed her chin, her cheeks, her eyelids—slow, deliberate kisses, and between each one, he repeated, "Marry me."

She recaptured his mouth and drew him into a deeper, wilder celebration.

He really hadn't needed to ask twice.

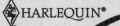

If you enjoyed what you just read,
then we've got an offer you can't resist!

Take 2 bestselling
love stories FREE!
Plus get a FREE surprise gift!

Clip this page and mail it to Harlequin Reader Service®

IN U.S.A.	IN CANADA
3010 Walden Ave.	P.O. Box 609
P.O. Box 1867	Fort Erie, Ontario
Buffalo, N.Y. 14240-1867	L2A 5X3

YES! Please send me 2 free Harlequin Temptation® novels and my free surprise gift. Then send me 4 brand-new novels every month, which I will receive months before they're available in stores. In the U.S.A., bill me at the bargain price of $3.12 plus 25¢ delivery per book and applicable sales tax, if any*. In Canada, bill me at the bargain price of $3.57 plus 25¢ delivery per book and applicable taxes**. That's the complete price and a savings of over 10% off the cover prices—what a great deal! I understand that accepting the 2 free books and gift places me under no obligation ever to buy any books. I can always return a shipment and cancel at any time. Even if I never buy another book from Harlequin, the 2 free books and gift are mine to keep forever. So why not take us up on our invitation. You'll be glad you did!

142 HEN CNEV
342 HEN CNEW

Name _____ (PLEASE PRINT)

Address _____ Apt.#

City _____ State/Prov. _____ Zip/Postal Code

* Terms and prices subject to change without notice. Sales tax applicable in N.Y.
** Canadian residents will be charged applicable provincial taxes and GST.
   All orders subject to approval. Offer limited to one per household.
   ® are registered trademarks of Harlequin Enterprises Limited.

TEMP99   ©1998 Harlequin Enterprises Limited

EXTRA! EXTRA!

The book all your favorite authors are raving about is finally here!

The 1999 Harlequin and Silhouette coupon book.

Each page is alive with savings that can't be beat!

Getting this incredible coupon book is as easy as 1, 2, 3.

1. During the months of November and December 1999 buy any 2 Harlequin or Silhouette books.

2. Send us your name, address and 2 proofs of purchase (cash receipt) to the address below.

3. Harlequin will send you a coupon book worth $10.00 off future purchases of Harlequin or Silhouette books in 2000.

Send us 3 cash register receipts as proofs of purchase and we will send you 2 coupon books worth a total saving of $20.00 (limit of 2 coupon books per customer).

Saving money has never been this easy.

Please allow 4-6 weeks for delivery. Offer expires December 31, 1999.

I accept your offer! Please send me (a) coupon booklet(s):

Name: _____

Address: _____ City: _____

State/Prov.: _____ Zip/Postal Code: _____

Send your name and address, along with your cash register receipts as proofs of purchase, to:

In the U.S.: Harlequin Books, P.O. Box 9057, Buffalo, N.Y. 14269

In Canada: Harlequin Books, P.O. Box 622, Fort Erie, Ontario L2A 5X3

Order your books and accept this coupon offer through our web site
http://www.romance.net
Valid in U.S. and Canada only.   PHQ4994R